Positive Thinking

Katie's last wish had come true. She *had* met somebody new on Saturday. And he was very nice, too. Now she had to forecast something wonderful for tomorrow — and make it come true before the end of the day!

Wistfully, Katie let her pen touch the blank page. Maybe there really was a fairy godmotherlike "romance" spirit who would mysteriously guide her hand when the words began to flow.

Katie took a deep breath and watched herself write. . . .

Other Scholastic paperbacks
you will enjoy:

A Royal Pain
by Ellen Conford

Acts of Love
by Maureen Daly

Hurricane Elaine
by Johanna Hurwitz

Just a Summer Romance
by Ann M. Martin

A, My Name Is Ami
by Norma Fox Mazer

The Summer of Mrs. MacGregor
by Betty Ren Wright

The Secret Diary of Katie Dinkerhoff

Lila Perl

AN
APPLE
PAPERBACK

SCHOLASTIC INC.
New York Toronto London Auckland Sydney

ISBN 0-590-41132-2

12 11 10 9 8 7 6 5 4 3 2 1   2   9/8 0 1 2 3 4/9

CHAPTER
1

On Tuesday, March 5, Katie Dinkerhoff wrote another big fat lie in her diary:

> *Had lunch today with T.P. and K.B., the two most popular girls in ninth grade. Who should stop by our table but R.G. He leaned over to say something to T.P. who'd called out to him. But all the time he kept looking at me. The next time I see him in study hall I'll walk right up to him and start talking. Why not!*

Katie slapped the covers of her navy-blue leatherette diary shut and turned the key to lock it. She didn't write in her diary every day, only when she needed a lift. And the lie she'd written today wasn't that terrible.

After all, Rob Garrett (R.G.) *had* stopped at Tracy Palowski and Kim Brewer's table. And Katie *had* been sitting there. Only thing was she'd been sitting a few places away. And she'd been eating lunch *not* with Tracy and Kim, but with Irma the Nerd.

Katie shoved the diary into her bureau drawer under a pile of itchy sweaters that Aunt Zoe had knitted for her and that she never wore. She could still see the wide-eyed look on Irma's face after Rob left and Tracy and Kim dissolved into some giggly conversation of their own.

"What *is* it?" Katie had snapped at Irma across the table. Katie was small and red-haired and could be hot-peppery at times, especially with Irma, who would drive anybody up the wall.

Irma grinned shyly. "He kept staring at you the whole time."

"I know," Katie whispered fiercely, not wanting to attract Tracy and Kim's attention to her anxious conversation with Irma. "Do you think I'm blind?"

Irma shook her head hard. "Oh, no, Katie," she said.

Katie watched Irma's short, straight, black hair swing out in a circle. Irma's hair always looked, Katie thought, as though it had been snipped even with the rim of a bowl. One day Katie was going to ask Irma if that was really the way she got her hair cut. Irma was new in school. She'd been hanging around Katie for about two weeks now. "Hanging around" was the right expression, too, Katie felt. Sort of like a boa constrictor draped threateningly across Katie's pale, slender shoulders.

"He was looking at you," Irma repeated insistently. "And I know why, too."

Katie blinked her eyes and licked her lips. Now and then Irma paid her a compliment in a way that seemed really sincere. Katie waited anxiously.

"There was something caught in your teeth braces," Irma went on after a moment's hesitation. "A big long shred of carrot. It was hanging out of your mouth like a . . . a fang. I . . . I'm sorry, Katie. That's what he was looking at."

Katie gasped, horrified. Her hand flew to her lips.

"Oh," Irma said, "it's gone now." She glanced down at the dish of carrot-and-raisin salad on Katie's lunch tray. "It fell out as soon as he left. It's probably sitting right back on top of the salad." That was Irma! She *would* have to tell every detail.

Katie could have killed her. "I don't believe you! I'd have felt something. If it was there, why didn't you let me know? Honestly, Irma. You're such a . . . nerd."

It was the first time Katie had called Irma that to her face, and she was shocked to hear herself say it. But it was what she had been thinking ever since Irma had turned up in Katie's homeroom and attached herself to Katie like a leech. Katie was going to have a harder time than ever now making other friends.

Irma was so strange, Katie thought, that she might have been a visitor from another planet doing a bad imitation of a modern, fourteen-year-old earthling. She wore brown leather oxfords and shapeless tweed skirts instead of sneakers and jeans like the other kids. She was clairvoyant at math, totally hung up about getting her library books back on time, and she flossed her teeth every day after lunch in the girls' bathroom — right in front of everyone. Weird,

Katie thought. That was the only word for her.

Irma hadn't seemed the least bit ruffled by Katie's outburst, though. Maybe she didn't know what a nerd was. Maybe she just didn't care. Maybe she couldn't afford to.

Katie leaned back against the assortment of counted-cross-stitch cushions on the studio bed in her long, narrow room. The cushions were another one of Aunt Zoe's projects. Katie sighed and told herself that the real reason she hadn't written in her diary about the carrot snagged in her braces was that *she* hadn't seen it. All she had was Irma's word for it.

For that matter, she had left Irma completely out of her diary, too. Not once had Katie mentioned her new friend in her recent entries. If the truth was nothing to brag about, why record it for posterity? The world of "ought-to-be" was so much more satisfying to write about, Katie thought. And maybe she really would talk to Rob Garrett the next time she saw him. At least he *had* noticed her.

Dum - dum - dum - dum . . . dum-dum-dum-dum-*dum*. Dum - dum - dum - dum. . . . Downstairs in the "ballroom," the music from Mr. Lloyd Huntziger's five P.M. tango lesson broke into Katie's daydream. She could hear the faint thump of the Latin dance rhythm vibrating upward through the floorboards and walls of the old Dinkerhoff house.

The fact that Katie's parents ran an old-fashioned dance studio for senior citizens was another thing Katie never mentioned in her diary. She could just see Babette, her mother, petite but wiry, subtly thrusting and pulling the balding and crease-necked

4

Mr. Huntziger around the dance floor. Katie wasn't especially thrilled at being known around Hooperville as the only child of a pair of fading ballroom-dancing teachers. Professionally, Katie's parents called themselves Babette and Raoul. But their real names were Betty and Ralph.

As a teenager, not much older than Katie was now, Betty-Babette had fallen in love with Ralph-Raoul, nearly ten years her senior, and soon gotten into Ralph's family's business, the Dinkerhoff dance studio. The broad, old-fashioned frame house, with its ballroom-studio on the ground floor, had been a landmark in Hooperville, in upstate New York, for three generations.

Babette, an enthusiastic convert to ballroom dancing and really good as both a dancer and a teacher, went on a crusade. Disco-type dancing might come and go, she declared. But the tango, the foxtrot, the rumba, the waltz — even the peabody — would go on forever.

In time Ralph's parents, Katie's grandparents, had retired and moved to Albuquerque. But the business hadn't died yet. Maybe that was because so many of Hooperville's ancient citizens still thought of themselves as twinkle-toed, so to speak.

What really worried Katie about the dance studio was Babette's insistence that one of these days the kids who were Katie's age were going to come back to ballroom dancing, "take lessons, have cotillions, just like they did right up through the nineteen-fifties, before rock-and-roll took over — "

"No way," Katie had shot back. "And please don't even *think* of having any handbills printed for me to give out around school. I'd die of em-

5

barrassment. Well . . . I just wouldn't do it."

Katie knew from experience that you had to stop Babette before she got started. She was a hustler. The things she'd promoted for Ralph and herself back in the early days! They had given paid dance demonstrations all over New York State and throughout the northeast. They'd entertained at clubs and big parties as often as once a week. And twice, before Katie was born, they'd gotten jobs on cruise ships — twelve days to the Bahamas — doing exhibitions and giving lessons on board. That was just after they'd won third prize in the Harvest Moon finals.

The thrumming of the music downstairs stopped abruptly and about two minutes later the doorknob of Katie's room turned with a sharp squeak.

Katie dived forward. She was supposed to be doing her algebra homework, not daydreaming lies to write in her diary and thinking of how uncomfortable it sometimes made her feel to be part of the has-been Dinkerhoff clan. To Katie, it seemed that her parents were living in the distant past, like a pair of extinct animals.

The door opened slowly. Bad news about Mr. Huntziger maybe. It wouldn't be the first time one of Babette's elderly clients began gasping for breath halfway through a private lesson.

Katie glanced up expectantly. It was Aunt Zoe. Her eyes behind her oversize glasses had a startled look, which wasn't exactly unusual.

"Anything wrong?" Katie inquired.

Zoe shook her head. "Should there be?"

"Well, the tango music stopped," Katie said. "I

thought maybe Mr. Huntziger . . . ran out of . . . steam."

Zoe pursed her lips to suppress a smile. "Oh honestly, Katie, you have such a vivid imagination. Lloyd Huntziger isn't that old. I even dated him once after his wife died. No, I only came up here to try one of my new ideas on you. I just want to get a quick gut reaction."

Zoe sidled around behind Katie's desk, which was backed up almost completely against the sliding door of Katie's clothes closet. No wonder Katie called her room "the sardine can." Luckily, Zoe was smallish, too. She was Katie's mother's sister and had lived with them ever since Katie could remember.

Zoe had been starting little home-based businesses on and off for years — custom-designed cold-weather clothing for pets; an emergency first-aid service for dying house plants; crocheted doorknob covers. And recently she'd even tried Zoe's Low-Calorie Brownies and Blondies, a mail-order brownie-baking business. But like all the others it started with high hopes and ended in grief or, in this case, in the garbage.

"You think I won't make a killing some day?" Zoe had challenged her sister and brother-in-law as they'd swept the last of the unordered, sawdust-flavored brownies into the trash. "I will. Just see if I don't."

"Hmmm . . . a new idea?" Katie mused. "Don't tell me. Let me guess. You're going to start a Chinese-food takeout business and call it Toh-mein Wok."

"My gosh!" Zoe exclaimed. "Ptomaine Wok. Oh

7

Katie, you're *terrible*! But listen, you're close. It *is* a takeout idea."

Zoe snuggled down onto the studio bed beside Katie. She clasped her hands together and hunched her shoulders. The huge orbs of her lenses closed in on Katie's face. "It's going to be a *health-food* takeout. Health food. What do you think of that?"

Katie acted like she didn't know what to think. But secretly she could already see another big flop in the making.

Zoe grabbed Katie's arm. "Let me explain, baby. Health food. It's good for you but it's a pain to cook. Right? All those ingredients — grains, rice, veggies, seeds, sprouts, nuts. Well, I've been stock-piling recipe ideas . . . Tofu Delight, Buddha's Bean-burgers, Soy Surprise. . . . Get it, Katie? Oh, please say you get it."

Katie got it, all right.

Ah, the dreamers who lived in the Dinkerhoff household, she thought to herself. Poor Aunt Zoe, all excited about one of her wacky brainstorms again. And Katie's parents, hoping to make the dance studio pay off by giving *free* demonstrations and luring old Mr. Huntziger and a bevy of Hooperville widows in for lessons. Didn't they realize that their "big" ideas were sure to fail? They might just as well have been beating a dead horse.

But *she*, Katie Dinkerhoff, had already made up her mind she wasn't going to fall into that trap. Aunt Zoe always said, "You gotta have a dream." Okay. Fine. Except that Katie was going to be sure to pick the *right* dream. *And* she'd make it come true, too.

Of course, she didn't know quite how just yet,

or even just what that dream would be. The only clue she had so far was the lies she wrote in her diary, the record of her secret life in which everything always worked out romantically . . . and beautifully. Katie firmly believed, though, that one of these days she was going to find *some* way of making her world of "ought-to-be" real.

CHAPTER 2

Irma was tailing Katie along the crowded school corridor between classes. She had an annoying habit of always walking just half a step behind Katie. If Katie slowed down so they could walk side by side, Irma slowed down, too. Typical nerdlike behavior, Katie told herself with a shake of her head.

"Oh, you just passed him!" Irma whispered suddenly into Katie's ear. "That's the third time this week. And he *still* looks at you every time." Irma nudged Katie's shoulder and chuckled. "Do you think he expects to see some vegetables stuck in your teeth?"

Katie stopped dead. "Irma, just quit it. Do you hear? You're not funny."

Irma gave Katie an embarrassed look.

It was bad enough that today was Friday and

Katie still hadn't gotten up the courage to speak to Rob Garrett as she'd promised to do in her diary entry on Tuesday. The problem was that every time she saw him she was with Irma, who stuck to her like flypaper. Irma was in every single one of Katie's classes, including study hall.

Katie had tried telling herself that maybe Rob Garrett wasn't even worth all the fuss. He had a loping walk and his cheeks were a little too pink. And he was only a ninth grader like Katie. But he was tall and good-looking and very popular with the other kids. It *would* be nice if she could get to know him better. . . .

And he did keep looking at her, as Irma said. But maybe he *was* just trying to see if anything new had gotten caught in her braces. Katie would hardly be able to carry on a conversation with him without showing her teeth. She'd already practiced talking to herself that way in front of the mirror. And she knew it didn't work.

Still . . . she wasn't giving up. She *was* going to talk to Rob the first chance she got, which meant whenever she could shake loose of Irma for about four minutes.

"Tomorrow's Saturday," Irma said almost apologetically as she and Katie settled themselves in their next class, which happened to be Spanish II.

Katie, still feeling peeved, nodded wordlessly.

"So why don't you and I do something? You know, plan to get together," Irma suggested.

Katie cringed inwardly and opened her Spanish book to avoid Irma's eyes. Five days a week of Irma for the past three weeks were enough. Now Irma was asking for six. Of course, it was nice to have a friend who was as doting as Irma. Katie hadn't had a really close friend since sixth grade, when Jennifer Small had moved away to Ithaca with her family. But Irma? . . . the weirdest girl in the school, who had a stranglehold like a boa constrictor and was as sticky as flypaper? What kind of a satisfying friendship was that?

"I can't," Katie whispered back as Señora McCardle entered the room and the class began to hush. "I'm always busy on Saturdays."

Irma raised her eyebrows and gave Katie a faintly curious smile. A little while later, she slid a note across her desk and onto Katie's.

Katie unfolded the note while Señora was writing on the blackboard.

"*¿Que haces los sábados?*" Irma had written.

Katie puzzled over the words for a moment. "What do you do on Saturdays?" they read. Wasn't that a little personal?

Katie thought of all sorts of answers like, "You sure are nosy," or "None of your business." But her Spanish wasn't as good as Irma's and she couldn't do the translation. So she ended up by writing, just beneath Irma's question, "*Es un secreto,*" and she passed the note back to Irma. It *was* a secret, too, Katie thought. Nothing she wanted to talk about.

Later that afternoon, walking Katie home from school, Irma said half-mournfully, "Well then, I guess you and I won't see each other until Monday. On Sunday we have to go visit my grandparents over in Binghamton. That's one of the reasons we moved here from Vermont, you know. To be closer to my mother's family."

Katie nodded. Irma had already told her how her father had recently changed jobs as an engineering consultant, how in Vermont they had lived way out in the country in a two-hundred-year-old farmhouse, how her mother was into weaving and breadbaking and things like that.

Katie and Irma slogged along silently through the frozen slush left over from the brief thawing of last week's snow. Just ahead of them, Katie's big house sat on the corner like a piece of bad news. Katie had resolved that she was going to keep Irma off her back on Saturdays. But there was no way she could have kept Irma from knowing about the Dinkerhoff dance studio. All of Hooperville knew. That was the whole point of the sign on the front porch that clearly said: BABETTE AND RAOUL — BALLROOM INSTRUCTION. In smaller letters were the names of the most popular dances Katie's parents taught and to the right, in silhouette, the dashing figures of a man and a woman twirling through the air.

Irma paused thoughtfully in front of the sign. "Me, I ought to take lessons. I've got two left feet. Think I could learn?"

Katie made a face. "Don't be silly, Irma. Kids our age don't take ballroom lessons. My parents teach mostly older folks." She was anxious to hurry Irma on her way. Imagine if Babette heard of a teenage kid who wanted to learn the waltz. She'd go on one of her feverish campaigns to round up every teenager in town. There'd be no stopping her.

But, of course, Irma hung on leechlike. "I'll bet it's fun just to watch. Your mother must be real

13

graceful. And your father's probably really handsome." Irma's eyes were lingering on the romantic silhouetted couple on the sign.

Katie didn't think of her parents or what they did as especially romantic at all. The talk around the big kitchen table where they had their meals was usually about money, or how to get more students, or about setting up prize contests and party nights at the studio. Babette's pretty features would pucker into a frown and the hanging lamp would beam down on Ralph's thinning hair as they mulled over their problems.

Katie cleared her throat. "Well, a lot of the lessons they give are private. So, you know, nobody is supposed to watch because it might make the student nervous."

Irma nodded and gave Katie an understanding smile. Katie felt a little stab of guilt. She had never asked Irma up to see her room even. But then she hadn't been to Irma's house yet, either. It just happened that Katie's house was on Irma's way to school. Or at least so Irma said.

"Um," Katie mumbled vaguely, "you'll have to stop in and look around one of these days." She promised herself she'd be sure to pick a time when her mother was out and the studio was empty. "I'll give you the fifty-cent tour." Right now Katie just wanted to see Irma take off. And with no more remarks about Saturday either.

But sure enough, just as Irma lifted her hand for her nerdlike wave, she said, "Have fun doing whatever you do tomorrow. And if you ever need anyone to do it with you, well, you know, I'd be . . . interested."

14

Katie waved back and dashed up the steps without answering. How could anybody have so little pride as Irma? Just imagine if she, Katie, went tagging along after girls like Tracy Palowski and Kim Brewer, begging them to be her friends, trying to be part of their crowd. Oh, she might *dream* of something like that in her diary. But in real life she could never go to the lengths Irma did to urge somebody, who'd been as off-putting as Katie, into spending time with her.

In fact, Katie decided, she'd have to be pretty careful about getting to where she was going tomorrow. She had a sneaking suspicion that Irma might be curious enough to try to follow her. She could actually imagine Irma hiding all morning behind a parked car across from the Dinkerhoff house, watching Katie finally come walking down the steps around lunchtime, and then darting from tree to tree along Chestnut Street, Market Street, Main Street, Broad Street, and Cavendish Avenue as she tracked Katie halfway across Hooperville to her no-longer-secret secret destination.

With someone like Irma you just never knew.

CHAPTER
3

When Katie arrived at the Sunnyside Nursing Home on Saturday afternoon, lunch trays were just being cleared from the tables at the far end of the main lounge, where some of the livelier residents ate their meals. She'd gotten to her secret destination all right without being followed — as far as she knew. But she was frozen stiff from the half-hour trek that zigzagged over to the part of town that lay on the other side of the business district. It was frigid out, with a skittish wind that hinted of spring but managed instead to send chilling jabs into every part of Katie's body.

As she usually did, Katie marched down the long corridor to the activities office to hang up her down jacket, wool cap, scarf, and gloves. By contrast to the outdoors, the temperature in the nursing home was toasty, even stifling. And the warmth blended, as it always did, with the odors of floor wax, bland cooked food, and strong disinfectant.

Jacqui Beamish, the young but portly activities director, was seated at her desk. "Oh, thank goodness you're here," she boomed in her deep contralto voice. "I've had two staff people out all week with the flu. Might be coming down with something myself, *and* we've got Bingo scheduled at two-fifteen. I could have used more than one volunteer this afternoon."

Katie winced inwardly, thinking of Irma, who would of course have been overjoyed to come with her. But she put the thought aside immediately. She just couldn't have Irma shadowing her everywhere she went, practically taking over her life.

Katie had been volunteering her Saturday afternoons at the Sunnyside Nursing Home for about three months now. She'd been more or less browbeaten into doing it by her mother. Babette and Raoul had given one of their free ballroom-dancing demonstrations at the Home back in October to entertain the residents, some of whom had actually been students of theirs at one time. Jacqui Beamish had asked Babette if she knew of any school kids who'd be willing to give some time to the ill and the elderly. And Babette had readily offered Katie.

Katie didn't mind really. Most of the people she helped out with were pleasant and gracious. A few were crochety and bossy, just like people anywhere. But Katie did draw the line at getting other kids from school to come to the Sunnyside with her on Saturday. Girls like Tracy Palowski and Kim Brewer hung out at football practice on Saturday afternoons. Or they went to the big new indoor shopping mall just outside town with its piped music, snack bars, and dozens of brightly lit shops to browse in. And, like a lot of the other stuff she left out of her diary, Katie had never written in it about being a junior volunteer at the Sunnyside Nursing Home. She wasn't "ashamed" of going there. It just wasn't part of her dream, her world of "ought-to-be."

"If you'd read to Mabel Delacorte for a while, that'd be great," Jacqui suggested. "I wheeled her into the sun room just before you came. Then, around two, you can help me set up for Bingo in the main lounge." Jacqui cleared her throat, making a trumpeting sound something like that of a bull elephant. "Yep, I'm definitely coming down with something bronchial." For such a healthy-looking person, Katie reflected, Jacqui Beamish carried on like a world-class hypochondriac nine-tenths of the time.

Obediently, Katie headed for the sun room, which got very little sun. It was filled with plants and old wicker furniture bathed in flickery neon lighting.

Sure enough, Mabel Delacorte was waiting in her wheelchair, her legs covered with a peach-colored afghan, her spidery, blue-veined hands clutching her newest romance novel.

"Oh goody," she cried out, as Katie entered the room, even though her eyesight was supposed to be terrible. "I just knew you'd come today, darling. Can't wait to get tucked into this one. *Love's Luscious Longing*, I think it's called."

Katie drew up a chair and took the glossy-covered paperback that Mrs. Delacorte held out to her. Mabel Delacorte was one of Katie's "regulars." She

18

was supposed to be ninety-one or ninety-two. But she had a beautician come in once a week to set her thinning snow-white hair into a cloud of spun sugar. She powdered her face and put on lipstick every day, and she had her nails lacquered in a color called Regency Pink.

"Mustn't ever let oneself go," Mrs. Delacorte was fond of saying. "I'm holding on to the dream, my dear, don't you know," she'd told Katie. Imagine, Katie thought, still having a dream in your nineties, confined to a wheelchair and living in a nursing home in Hooperville, New York. She supposed that Mrs. Delacorte's dreams were somehow connected with the romances Katie read to her. The stories were silly and improbable . . . even worse, impossible. But they apparently came to life in Mabel Delacorte's head and took on a vivid, Technicolor reality.

Katie examined the book, letting her eyes roam briefly over the first page. Then she started reading to Mrs. Delacorte out loud.

This one opened on a wild Caribbean island that had just been invaded by Barbary pirates. The heroine, her bosom heaving, watched the landing of the swashbuckling bandits from her family's ruined hilltop plantation house. It was only a matter of time now before the pirate captain began slashing his way up through the tangled greenery to the veranda. There the heroine waited, proud and hostile, her late father's loaded pistol clutched in both hands, aimed to fire in defense of her honor. . . .

Katie read on, getting rather interested herself and thinking how much Mabel Delacorte must be loving this new story.

"Z-z-z-z-z humff . . . z-z-z-z-z humff . . . z-z-z-z-z-z-z . . ."

Katie, who was on page five, looked up from her reading. A few other residents who appeared to be asleep were sitting in the sun room. But the snoring seemed to be coming from right beside Katie. Sure enough, Mabel Delacorte, although she was sitting stark upright, had fallen into a deep snooze.

Katie was surprised and a little embarrassed. Mrs. Delacorte had never done that before. Katie had *tried* to read with expression and liveliness. And the story certainly didn't seem to be boring so far.

Katie looked around the room sheepishly. A bright-eyed woman who had wheeled herself almost directly opposite them stared at Katie and nodded her head rhythmically as if to say, "See, that's the way it goes."

At first Katie thought the woman was offering a touch of friendly sympathy. But after a while Katie realized that her head wasn't going to stop shaking.

Mabel Delacorte went on dozing noisily. Maybe she was already dreaming the opening scene that Katie had read to her. Katie glanced down at the book and decided to take a look at the last page. She knew, from experience, that the story would end gloriously with the heroine being swept away in the pirate's arms. It would turn out that he wasn't a real pirate, of course. He was the scion of royalty, come to claim his true inheritance, which had been buried many years ago by ignoble enemies beneath the moldering ruins of the island's old stone fortress. Or some such thing.

Satisfied that she had been right about the happy ending, Katie swept past the final page. As she did so, her fingers brushed against a stiff card that was bound into the book between the last page and the back cover. The card, she noticed, was detachable. You could remove it simply by tearing it out along a row of perforations. Faintly curious, Katie turned the book sideways and read the card:

> Be sure to enter our *Romantic Couples Contest*, Teen or Adult Division. See below for prizes and details.

With Mrs. Delacorte still sleeping and the woman with the shaking head still staring at her, Katie went on to examine the fine print under the announcement.

It seemed the romance-novel publisher of the book Katie had been reading was holding a contest to pick the most romantic-looking real-life couple. All you had to do to enter was to send in a photo of the two of you and tell in fifty words or less how you met and how it feels to be part of a couple. The first prize in the teen division was a fully-chaperoned, all-expense-paid, "romantic adventure weekend" in New York City.

As she glanced over the contest rules, Katie couldn't help thinking how all the thrilling details of winning such a contest would look in the pages of her diary. Imagine being able to tell about flying down to New York, being transported from the airport to your hotel in a shiny black limo, being interviewed at the romance publisher's office with flash guns popping and TV cameras going, and then "doing" the town — the bright lights of Broadway, the views from the city's skyscrapers, a ferry ride to the Statue of Liberty, a carriage ride through Central Park. . . .

"Ah, there you are." A voice startled Katie from the doorway of the sun room. It was Jacqui Beamish and the clock on the wall read nearly two P.M., time to help set up the afternoon's Bingo game.

Her fingers still on the contest-announcement card, Katie jumped to her feet. "Coming," she called out hastily to Jacqui. Undisturbed, Mabel Delacorte continued to "z-z-z-z-z humff" in her chair. Gently, Katie leaned over to tuck the paperback book in alongside Mrs. Delacorte. But at the last moment, on an impulse that surprised even herself, Katie pulled back, tore out the card along its perforated edges, and slipped it into the pocket of her jeans. Then, carefully placing *Love's Luscious Longing* between Mrs. Delacorte's peach afghan and the padded side of her wheelchair, Katie tiptoed softly out of the sun room.

All that afternoon, as Katie called out the numbers for the Sunnyside Nursing Home Bingo game, she couldn't stop thinking about the Romantic Couples Contest.

"B fifteen," Katie announced, silently telling herself that of course she didn't stand one chance in a zillion of winning. "N forty-three," Katie sang out, thinking that, on the other hand, if you were going to pursue a dream why not make it a great one like spending the most romantic weekend of your life in glamorous New York City with a very special person.

"G fifty," Katie ventured. Even Aunt Zoe, who believed so strongly that "You gotta have a dream," would have told Katie she was crazy to take on this one. But then again, look what Katie's mother and father had accomplished when they were young. They had won an important prize in a nationwide dance competition and ended up going on not one but two fantastic cruises.

"O seventy — " Katie had opened her mouth to report the next number. But at that moment a faint elderly voice from across the room called out, "Bingo!"

Katie looked up and snapped back to reality. Jacqui Beamish had already risen and was on her way to fetch the winning card from the silver-haired man who sat with his hands resting on the walker parked in front of his chair.

Bingo, Katie told herself wryly, as she stopped the game until Jacqui could check the winner's card for possible mistakes. What am I even thinking of? A couple, romantic or otherwise, means two. *Two* people. Who in the narrow little world of Hooperville is the other half of *my* couple?

CHAPTER
4

On Monday afternoon, Katie climbed the steps of the Dinkerhoff dance studio with Irma in tow.

"I can only stay a minute," Irma remarked as Katie unlocked the big front door. But even as Katie stepped over the threshold, she could feel Irma behind her faintly pushing at her shoulder with eagerness.

"Oh," Irma gasped, breathing hard. They were in the high-ceilinged, dimly lit front hall. To the left were the massive sliding doors that opened into the studio. Irma tiptoed toward the pulled-together doors and put one ear to the crack where they met.

She smiled at Katie. "It's quiet in there."

"I know," Katie retorted. "Monday's a slow day. No afternoon classes. Ever."

Of course, Katie had worked all this out in advance. She knew that her mother, Babette, wouldn't be around. On Mondays, Babette drove over to Binghamton to do exercise workouts at the studio of a friend of hers. And Ralph, who did a little insurance selling on the side, would be out seeing customers. Katie often thought of her mother as "Babette," but she had never been able to see her father as "Raoul."

Katie tossed her jacket and school books on the carved-oak hall table and motioned to Irma to do the same.

"Come on," she said, advancing toward the ballroom doors. "I'll give you a peek at the studio."

"Ooh," Irma trilled, without even having seen inside yet.

Katie gave the door on the right a hard wrench. It squeaked, groaned, and then slid away from her. There was the ballroom, looking gloomy and immense in the faint light that came through the blinds and drapes of the windows that faced onto the wraparound front porch. Before Irma could say anything, Katie switched on a few lights including the big crystal chandelier that brought the polished wood floor to life and sent diamond-shaped sparkles into the deepest recesses of the room.

This seemed to leave Irma entirely speechless. Not making a sound, she slowly ventured toward the center of the room in her baggy skirt and broad-toed brown leather oxfords. She really was, Katie thought to herself, like somebody from another planet. Well, certainly like somebody from another part of the century — maybe the nineteen-thirties, as they appeared in old movies that were rerun on late-night TV.

25

While Katie watched from the sidelines, Irma stopped directly beneath the glowing chandelier. She crossed her arms tightly against her chest and gazed around her in rapture. Yes, Katie told herself, the scene was getting to look more and more like one of those sentimental old movies in which a gawky young girl, destined for stardom, finds herself on the glittering stage of a deserted theater for the first time in her life.

"Irma," Katie called out almost sharply. "Are you okay? Do you want to come upstairs and see my room?" Katie figured one fast look at "the sardine can" would jolt Irma back into the world of the living.

But before Irma could answer, Katie heard her own name called. She turned and saw Aunt Zoe standing almost directly behind her, one hand on her heart in a gesture of just-relieved fright.

"Katie," Zoe panted. "I didn't know you were out here. What are you do—?" Zoe had just caught sight of Irma. "What? . . . I mean *who* . . . is that?" Even Zoe must have been struck by Irma's unusual appearance.

"It's Irma," Katie replied, perfectly aware that she had never mentioned her nerdy friend at home, any more than she had ever written about Irma in her diary. "She's . . . um . . . someone from school."

By this time Irma had come out of her trance and was beginning to come toward them with a hesitating walk and a semi-apologetic smile on her lips.

"Oh, Mrs. Dinkerhoff," Irma exclaimed, directly approaching Zoe, "I've heard so much about you and your wonderful ballroom lessons. Katie said I could come and look at the studio. It's thrilling, this big old-fashioned house and this beautiful — "

Aunt Zoe was shaking her head. "No, no dear. I'm afraid you've got it wrong. I'm not Katie's mother. I'm her aunt. I don't teach ballroom. I'm in the health-food takeout business."

Zoe turned impulsively to Katie. "You came at a good time. I'm in the kitchen mixing up a whole bunch of gorp to put in my health-cookie recipe. You and . . . Irma . . . can be my guinea pigs."

"Gorp?" Katie made a face. "Sounds awful. Sort of like glop. What is it?"

"Oh, it's delicious," Irma said with enthusiasm. "It's like trail mix — nuts, seeds, dried fruit. We snack on it all the time at our house."

Aunt Zoe, who was a little taller than Katie (everybody was) but not much taller than Irma, looked at Irma fondly. "A person after my own heart. At least *you* know what I'm talking about. Everybody else around here thinks I'm crazy. Come on. Come in the kitchen. I'll show you."

Forty-five minutes later, Aunt Zoe and Irma were still jawing away about health food at the kitchen table. Katie remembered too late that Irma's mother was the homespun type who baked her own bread and had even churned her own butter when they'd lived in the Vermont farmhouse. And looking around in boredom, while Irma and Zoe compared the merits of mung-bean sprouts versus alfalfa sprouts, Katie realized that the springy mustard-and-brown cloth of Irma's shapeless wool skirt had probably been hand woven on Irma's mother's loom. Who would have thought that Irma was going to have so much in common with a member of Katie's family?

"Irma," Katie interrupted, chewing absently on a mouthful of raisin-and-sunflower-seed gorp from the big bowl in the middle of the table, "shouldn't you call your mother?"

Irma hardly looked up. "Oh, it's okay. She knows where I am."

Katie could feel a few licks of angry fire in her cheeks. She could clearly recall Irma saying about an hour ago, "I can only stay a minute." And how did Irma's mother "know" where she was when Katie had only invited Irma that afternoon in school?

"Well," Katie said, getting to her feet, "I can't speak for you two. But *I've* got homework to do."

Aunt Zoe glanced up, her eyes slightly anxious through her big lenses. "Irma's just going to write down her phone number, Katie. She says she thinks her mother can help me with some recipes for my takeout business. I can't thank you enough, Katie, for having brought Irma home today. And I'm sure we're going to see a lot more of her."

Katie felt sure of it, too. And a lot of good that was going to do *her*.

"I'll go get your coat, Irma," Katie mumbled, heading for the front hall.

Irma finished writing down her number for Aunt Zoe and scrambled to her feet. She looked back gratefully at Zoe and then dutifully called after Katie, "I'll come with you, Katie. Guess I really should be going."

As soon as they were out in the front hall, Katie realized she'd left the lights on in the ballroom. Babette would be angry. They were trying to watch expenses until "things picked up a little."

Katie quickly ran her hand down the panel of

wall switches, plunging the studio into darkness — and not a moment too soon. While Irma was still wriggling her arms into the sleeves of her coat and telling Katie how much she liked her family so far, Katie heard rapid footsteps on the front porch. The next instant the front door opened with a sharp click and there stood Katie's mother, her car keys dangling from one hand and a small bag of groceries in the other.

Katie thought Babette wore a slightly pained expression until she saw Irma. Then she put on her "public" face and brightened up with anticipation.

"How come you're so early?" Katie pounced. This was exactly the meeting she'd been hoping to avoid.

"Early?" Babette asked absently. "Not really. It's past four. And who is your friend, Katie? I saw the lights on in the studio from outside." So Katie hadn't put them out in time after all.

Katie introduced Irma. "I was giving her a quick look around the house," Katie explained. "But she's just leaving." She wanted to hustle Irma past Babette. The faster the better.

Babette put down her package and took off her cream-colored fake-fur jacket. Catlike, she circled Irma, who was smiling with genuine pleasure at meeting Katie's mother at last.

"So you've just seen our ballroom," Babette ventured. "You must be new in town. I know everybody. Well, almost. You see, we've been in business here such a long time."

Irma nodded but didn't speak. She couldn't seem to take her eyes off Katie's mother. Babette's blonde hair was tousled and her makeup slightly smudged.

But she had an aura of oldtime movie-star glamour about her. Babette cultivated that look and called it her "image." She said her clients expected it.

Finding her tongue at last, Irma explained that her family had only been living in Hooperville about a month. "It must be wonderful to be able to do all those dances like it says on the sign outside," she babbled on admiringly as she took her time buttoning up her coat.

Katie felt like lifting Irma up bodily and tossing her out the front door.

Babette smiled warmly. "Oh, they're not at all hard to learn, especially if you start young. And ballroom dancing opens up a lifetime of healthy fun and interesting social contacts. I have students of all ages. I guess Katie's told you."

Irma glanced slyly at Katie, a look that Babette caught.

"Oh, I know Katie doesn't think today's kids would be interested in learning the waltz or even the fox-trot. But I think she's wrong." Babette cocked her head in Katie's direction. "And one of these days I'm going to prove it."

Katie glared at her mother. She'd known this was coming. Next thing, Babette would be offering Irma a trial lesson, absolutely free, hoping of course to use Irma as bait to lure the other kids Katie went to school with. Babette was desperate all right. Did she really think anybody would follow the example of such an obvious nerd as Irma?

Katie put one arm firmly around the back of Irma's waist. "She really has to go now, Mom. She was only *supposed to stay a minute*." With each emphasized word, Katie gave Irma a meaningful jab just to the right of her backbone.

Obediently, Irma began to bow her way out. "Yes, I guess I do have to go. But it was wonderful meeting you, Mrs. Dinkerhoff," she said lingeringly. "And I sure *would* like to learn the waltz some time."

Leave it to Irma. She always managed to get in the last word. Babette wasn't going to forget the opening Irma had just given her! And it was sure to cause trouble for Katie.

The moment she had locked the front door on Irma, Katie raced past her mother mumbling something about "tons of homework" and galloped upstairs.

She closed the door of her room behind her, leaped up onto her bed, and sat crouched over her raised knees, her hands clawing her forehead.

Katie just didn't know what she was going to do about Irma, who had a real talent for crawling onto the scene and messing things up for her. And all the while Katie had something much more challenging on her mind, something she really needed to concentrate on. Ever since Saturday, it had been gnawing at her thoughts, stirring her imagination with visions of shimmering excitement . . . the Romantic Couples Contest!

On a sudden impulse — maybe because she was so fed up with Irma — Katie leaned over, opened her itchy-sweater drawer, and took out her diary. She hadn't written in it for nearly a week.

Katie opened it to her last entry, the one about promising herself to speak to Rob Garrett, who'd kept looking at her in the lunchroom on Tuesday, March 5.

Then she did an odd thing. Even though today

31

was only Monday, March 11, Katie marked the heading of her entry "Tuesday, March 12." That was tomorrow.

Pausing just for a second, she bent her head over the page and wrote:

> *Today I got rid of Irma and I actually went over and talked to Rob Garrett. I also sent away for the application blank to enter the Romantic Couples Contest, Teen Division!*

Katie slapped the diary shut the way she always did. Only this time she hadn't written a lie in it. Tomorrow, Tuesday, March 12, she would see to it that what she had written became the truth.

No more lies! Katie Dinkerhoff would dare herself to make her world of "ought-to-be" real. And, for a start, she was going to do everything she could to make her dream of being in the Romantic Couples Contest come true.

CHAPTER
5

"Irma," Katie said urgently the next afternoon, "you've got to help me out."

They were on their way to study hall, which never settled down for the first ten minutes or so because Mr. Burnside, the teacher-in-charge, always got there late.

"What?" Irma asked, responding to the tense note in Katie's voice.

Katie dumped three library books into Irma's arms and placed her library card on the top book. "Please take these back to the library for me. This one can be returned. This one needs to be renewed. And this one I want to keep but I need volume two of it, so here's volume one so you'll know what to look for."

Irma's arms sank under the weight.

"Oh, here," Katie added quickly. "I'll take *your*

books to study hall with me so you won't have so much to carry up the stairs." She reached underneath the pile for Irma's textbooks and notebook. The school library was up on the fifth floor and she and Irma were down on the second.

Irma still looked confused.

"But why can't *you* go, Katie? I mean, I don't *mind*. But it's okay to take library time out of study-hall period. We could even go together."

"I *can't*," Katie said, breathing hard. "I never finished my Spanish homework. And that's next period. Don't you see I haven't got any time to waste?"

Irma smiled helpfully. "I could lend you mine to copy. That would speed things up."

"No!" Katie insisted. She knew there was an edge of panic in her voice. Her cheeks must have been as red as her hair by now. And her mouth was so dry her braces felt like hot metal. "It'll speed things up a *lot* more if you'll do me this favor."

With that, Katie dashed off down the corridor. Irma wouldn't dare follow her. She was totally compulsive about anything having to do with the returning or renewing of library books. And of course Katie figured that just traipsing up and down the three flights of stairs was bound to take Irma a while.

At the door of the study hall, a kind of small assembly room with a stage, Katie paused to feel for the arrangement of her hair and make sure it was framing her face the way it was supposed to. Then she licked her lips with her tongue, which felt like cotton, and marched as confidently as she could into the room.

What if Rob Garrett wasn't even there today? Suppose he had the flu or had been hit in the face with a hockey puck? Katie *had* to talk to him. She had vowed not to write any more stupid lies in her diary. She was supposed to make what she had written for today true.

A dozen or so kids had already arrived, tossed their books on various seats, and were rambling around just letting off steam. Katie's eyes darted across the room in a frenzy. Then she saw him. He was standing at the end of a row of seats, partly blocked by two other boys.

Rob was doing something with his hands and concentrating on something in the air. As Katie watched, she saw two red-and-blue beanbaglike cubes go flying upward past Rob's face. They came down and two more went up. Katie put her and Irma's books down on the nearest two seats and threaded her way toward Rob and the two boys.

It wasn't as hard as she'd expected it to be. The fact that Rob was practicing juggling and already had a small audience made her going up to him seem more natural. And, after all, it didn't say in her diary that *he* had to talk to her, only that *she* had talked to him — although Katie didn't suppose there was much point in a one-way conversation in which Rob remained silent the whole time.

Hunching her shoulders, Katie slipped in alongside one of the boys and stationed herself in front of Rob, her knuckles resting on her waist.

Rob was juggling three cubes at once. "Hey, you're pretty good," Katie exclaimed after a while, as Rob kept the colored cubes rotating in the air.

But at the very moment that Katie spoke, Rob's

eyes lost their concentration and he missed. All three cubes fell on the floor with a soft thud.

The two boys watching Rob looked at Katie with annoyance. She knew her voice had come out squeaky and too high-pitched. She could feel her cheeks flame by another fifteen degrees at least.

"Oops, sorry," Katie apologized, looking around her for some sign of forgiveness. But nobody said a word. Rob picked up the juggling cubes and started again, slowly. The first time out, though, he missed again.

One of the other boys grabbed the three cubes. "Nah, nah. Ya gonna look around or juggle, Garrett? It takes concentration. Like this, see?"

The other boy was clearly better at juggling. Rob stuck his hands in his pockets and watched. Several minutes went by in which Katie, completely ignored, wished she could sink through the floor. Rob finally swiveled around and looked at her.

"See what you made me do, pipsqueak?" he said. "I don't know why they let seventh graders into ninth-grade study hall anyway."

Katie looked around her in disbelief. "What seventh graders?"

Rob began to laugh in a slightly embarrassed way. "You," he said. "Okay, *maybe* you're an eighth grader. *Maybe*, though I doubt it."

Katie felt her temper flare. "*You* think I'm a seventh grader?" she demanded. "What makes you think that? I can't believe you're serious."

Things weren't going at all the way Katie had hoped they would. If this was Rob's idea of friendly teasing, she didn't like it at all. Rob, whom she had once actually sort of admired — even considered as the *possible* other half of a teen couple — was behaving like a big jerk. The only positive thing was that . . . well, she *was* talking to him. She hadn't lied to her diary.

Rob raised one shoulder. "Of course I'm serious. Well, just look at yourself. First of all, you're only about four feet tall. Second of all, you've still got braces. My kid sister's got braces. We call her metalmouth. Or sometimes, railroad tracks . . ."

Katie had reached the boiling point by now. "And thirdly?" she snarled at him.

Rob raised his head and looked past her. "Thirdly, there's that klutzy-looking friend of yours that just came in the room. Now don't tell me *she's* more than a seventh grader. Tall for her age, maybe. But . . ." Rob began to shake his head back and forth as if no words could describe Irma the Nerd.

Katie turned around and saw Irma craning her neck, like a worried bird, in search of Katie. Then Irma caught sight of her and triumphantly held up the library books she'd brought back for Katie. Mission accomplished.

Katie waved wanly. She hadn't expected Irma back so soon. She was supposed to be frantically trying to finish her Spanish homework. Now she'd have to explain to Irma what had been going on with her and Rob. One thing, though. Katie wouldn't tell Irma that he had called her a klutz. That was *too* mean. Rob's words made Katie realize that she had a spark of loyalty toward Irma, and this surprised her.

"You're pretty sick, Rob Garrett," Katie shot at him over her shoulder as she started toward Irma. Mr. Burnside had just entered the room and the study-hall kids, who now numbered around forty, were scrambling into their places.

Rob shuffled behind her toward his own seat. "Temper, temper," he clucked softly. "You'd be cute, redhead, if you'd just grow up a little."

The moment Katie sat down, Irma poked her hard. "You were talking to *him*," she whispered.

Katie shook her head back and forth emphatically. "Please don't say another word, Irma. He's awful, just awful. I'm *never* talking to him again."

"Why?" Irma persisted. "What did he say to you?"

Katie didn't reply. She began to look through one of the library books that Irma had brought back.

Irma poked her again. "I thought you were going to finish your Spanish homework in study hall. Isn't that why you were in such a hurry to get here?"

Katie fidgeted. "I did . . . uh . . . some before you got back. It's just about finished now." Actually, Katie had finished all her Spanish homework at home the night before.

Irma looked at her quizzically and a sly grin began to spread across her face. Irma had caught on to what Katie had been trying to do — ditch Irma and talk to Rob Garrett alone. "Gee," Irma said, "I wish you'd tell me what happened while I was gone. I hurried all the way upstairs to the library for you and got you everything you wanted. . . ."

"Irma," Katie hissed between clenched teeth, "will you *please* leave me alone. I'm just sick of your sticking to me like glue and wanting to know every little thing." Katie's voice rose higher and higher. She was furious with Rob and she was taking it out on Irma, which she knew was wrong. But she just couldn't help herself. If she started to tell Irma what Rob had said, she might not be able to keep from blurting out his remark about Irma. Why *did* Irma have to be so nosy?

Before Katie realized it, she was squawking hoarsely over the occasional buzzes of conversation in the generally hushed study hall, while Irma beside her remained totally silent.

"*You.*" Mr. Burnside was standing in the aisle at the end of her row and pointing a blunt finger at Katie. He was a tall man with a thatch of gray hair and severe horn-rimmed glasses. "What's the argument about?" he inquired wearily.

Irma looked up innocently. "No argument, Mr. Burnside," she said. Katie gulped with embarrassment at Irma's being so protective of her. She could have put the blame on Katie, but she didn't.

Katie felt so awful about everything that she knew she had to get out of there. "I . . . I don't feel too well," she said, half rising from her seat. "May I leave the room?"

"Take a pass from the platform," Mr. Burnside said in a bored voice. "And be *sure* to be back here before the end of the period. No wandering around the building."

Without daring to so much as glance at Irma, Katie got up and wriggled past the row of seats to the aisle. A few kids who'd heard her exchange with Mr. Burnside looked up. The teacher had already moved away to the back of the room.

Sheepishly, Katie walked to the front and picked up one of the plastic-encased passes that sat on the rim of the study-hall stage. She turned and went quickly up the aisle toward the door at the back, trying not to look left or right.

Suddenly a large sneakered foot shot out of one of the rows on her left side. Katie saw it just in time, jolting backward and breaking her stride. She just managed to avoid tripping. Then she sped past the person who had put his foot out, without even looking up.

She didn't need to. Katie remembered that sneaker all too clearly. The last time she'd seen it was when Rob Garrett had dropped all three of his colored juggling cubes on the floor and she had stared down at them lying at his feet.

In the girls' bathroom, which was happily empty, Katie took one look in the mirror and began to splash cold water on her burning cheeks. Her eyes were feverishly bright, too. Maybe she was coming down with something.

She hoped so. She couldn't face anybody, not even herself. And she felt terrible about having sounded so mean to Irma, who was probably her only real friend. What a mess she'd made of everything with her dumb, boastful diary entry that *had* to become a reality. She hadn't done a halfway job either. To make matters worse, she'd mailed away only that morning for an application blank to enter the Romantic Couples Contest.

CHAPTER
6

"Is everybody ready for my Green-Revolution Casserole?" Aunt Zoe called out cheerfully as she leaned across the open oven door, her hands encased in oversize mitts.

Katie and her parents were already seated at the large round table in the big Dinkerhoff kitchen.

"I hate to tell you what the word 'green' does to me," Katie remarked. "Do you have to call it that?"

Katie caught her father's eye and they exchanged a conspirational look. Ralph wasn't too thrilled either with having to eat Zoe's health-food experiments, which had been coming to the table at dinnertime for over a week now. But since Babette seldom cooked and Ralph was mainly an outdoor summertime chef, the Dinkerhoffs didn't have much choice.

"Ahh, Katie," Zoe said, lugging the steaming

41

earthenware dish to the table, "gimme a break, huh?" She set the food down on a heat-proof mat and lifted one mitted hand to wipe her forehead.

"Smells . . . interesting, Zoe," Babette said supportively. "I'm sure it's full of all sorts of good things."

"Of course it is!" Zoe exclaimed, pulling up her own chair and starting to dole out gigantic portions of what looked mainly like gluey gray rice with specks of carrot-colored vegetables in it.

"It isn't green at all," Katie murmured, trying to draw her plate away before the last gloppy mound fell from the serving spoon. "What kind of a revolution did you say it was?"

"Green, green," Zoe replied impatiently. "You can bet your friend Irma and her mother would know what I was talking about. The Green Revolution had to do with a whole new way of growing rice and wheat and stuff so people in poor countries would have more food to — "

"That reminds me," Babette broke in, turning to Katie with her mouth slightly full. "How *is* your friend Irma? You know," she added, looking pointedly across the table at Ralph, "I thought that child had *real* possibilities."

Katie gave her mother a suspicious glance. "Possibilities for what?"

"Oh," Babette said airily, "all sorts of things." She turned to Katie's father again, "Katie's new friend really seemed interested in ballroom. She actually said she wanted to learn the — "

Katie, who had just taken a large sip from a glass beside her plate, suddenly began to cough and choke.

Zoe leaped to her feet and began to pound Katie on the back.

"No, no. Not that way," Ralph said. He got up quickly and came around behind Katie's chair. He leaned over. "Food caught in your throat, princess?"

Katie shook her head. It was nothing really, just some liquid that had started to go down the wrong pipe. She was already getting her breath back. At least her timing had been good. She'd kept Babette from saying the word "waltz."

Ralph went back to his place and Zoe and Babette breathed sighs of relief. "Serves you right for drinking some terrible cola concoction while eating my nourishing food, Katie," Zoe said. "You should know the two don't go together."

Katie was silent and exchanged another look with her father. Ralph was quietly drinking something from a tall silver-colored mug with his dinner. Katie suspected it wasn't water.

"Well, anyway," Babette went on, "if you don't want me to suggest anything having to do with the studio for Irma — and I can see that you don't — I have another thought I hope you'll hear me out on."

Katie got down one more mouthful of Zoe's Green Revolution and steeled herself for the next onslaught.

"It's about Jacqui Beamish over at the nursing home. I ran into her downtown this afternoon. Katie, she's absolutely begging for more teenage volunteers. She says you're doing such a good job. Surely you can find a classmate or two to bring along on Saturdays. So I thought of Irma."

Katie clunked her fork down onto her plate. "You didn't actually tell her about Irma," she said angrily.

Babette looked surprised at Katie's reaction. "Well, no, I didn't mention her name. I just said I'd talk to you because you had a friend and I was pretty sure — "

"Well, you had no right to . . . to . . ."

Zoe leaned over and put a restraining hand on Katie's arm. "Honey, why are you so down on Irma? I had the nicest talk with her mother this week on the telephone. She actually suggested most of the ingredients that I put into this very dish you're eating."

Katie rolled her eyes.

"Well," Zoe went on, "what I'm trying to say is if Irma's a friend why don't you treat her like one?"

Katie gave both Zoe and her mother a look of exasperation. "I wish you would all get this straight. Irma *is* a friend . . . sort of. But I didn't pick her. She picked me. The . . . the trouble is everybody around school thinks she's a . . . a nerd. And, well, because she hangs around me all the time, the . . . the other kids won't have anything to do with me."

Katie could feel herself beginning to choke up. Every time she'd seen Rob Garrett in school since he'd pegged her and Irma as a pair of seventh graders, she'd been stuck as usual with Irma. Of course, Katie wasn't talking to Rob anymore. Ever. So it didn't really matter about him. But what about the rest of the school?

Just the other day, Irma had sat down for lunch again at Kim Brewer and Tracy Palowski's table. When Katie had followed with her tray, she'd seen

44

the two girls whispering and the sly grins on their faces as they watched Irma settle herself a couple of seats away from them.

Immediately Katie had veered off and sat down somewhere else. Then she had to make elaborate signals with her hands every time Irma looked up to get Irma to move.

"Why didn't you want me to sit there?" Irma whispered after she'd finally switched over. "You used to like that table."

Katie didn't answer.

"Oh, I get it," Irma said. "You're worried that *he* might come around to talk to them. And you're real mad at him, even though you still never told me what he said that day in study hall."

It was true, Katie had refused to talk to Irma about her conversation with Rob. There were two reasons, really. One was that she was never going to tell Irma that Rob had called her a klutz. And the other reason was that Katie just couldn't share her humiliation, not even with Irma. Katie *was* a secretive kind of person, she supposed. As long as Irma seemed to go along with that goodnaturedly, Katie wasn't going to openly admit the awful truth. After all, she'd even told lies to her diary to make things look better!

Katie pushed her chair back and got up from the supper table. "I'm . . . um . . . just not hungry anymore."

Zoe and Babette exchanged glances. They both seemed at a loss for words since Katie's outburst about Irma's constant presence keeping the other kids away from her. Maybe they were both remembering their own school days, when being friends with the one girl in the class who was "different" could really cut down on your popularity.

With a sidelong glance at Katie, Zoe turned to Babette. "Katie's braces are probably going to come off sometime this year. Right?"

Babette nodded. "That's what Dr. Evans said on our last visit. Christmas maybe."

"Oh, big deal," Katie commented, realizing that Zoe was just trying to cheer her up. "Practically a whole year. And then," she mimicked, "I'll change over from an ugly duckling to a swan. Yum, yum. I can hardly wait." Katie's orthodontist, Dr. Evans, kept all his teenage girl patients happy — or so he thought — by promising them such miracles.

Katie's father, who was determinedly finishing off the food on his plate with the help of whatever was in the tall silver mug, glanced up with a faint look of concern. Katie could see that she was making everybody uncomfortable. But did anybody understand her feelings? And now this talk of Babette making promises to Jacqui Beamish.

Zoe reached across the table to remove the casserole. "I'm sorry nobody liked my health-food experiment very much. Maybe I can jazz it up next time with some cashew nuts and a handful of pomegranate seeds. But listen, let's not blame *this* on Irma, too."

At the mention of Irma's name, Katie turned to her mother again. "Just don't go telling people what I will or won't do. Please. Maybe now you can see that if I don't want to take Irma everyplace with me, I have my reasons. And that goes for Saturdays at the nursing home, too."

Babette shrugged, looking slightly hurt. "Do as you like, Katie, by all means."

Babette's quiet sarcasm was the last straw. It always infuriated Katie more than the worst yelling and screaming.

"*Ohhh!*" Katie growled. She left the room in a huff. Nothing was going right for her. Nothing.

CHAPTER 7

About twenty minutes after she'd dashed up-stairs, Katie's father knocked on the door of her room. She was sprawled on the bed surrounded by Spanish verbs.

Ralph tiptoed in, one finger sheepishly pressed to his lips, and went and sat in Katie's only chair. He leaned back and folded his hands behind his head. "Feeling better, princess?"

"Not especially," Katie said, just starting to fill in a homework study-sheet of the past-perfect tenses of regular verbs ending in *ar*. She and her father had often had private talks in the past. But lately there hadn't been too many of them. Katie didn't know if it had something to do with the fact that she was getting older or simply because Ralph was putting more and more time into his on-the-side insurance business. He was out nearly all day and most evenings when there weren't lessons to give at the studio.

"Well," Ralph began a little awkwardly as he leaned forward and clasped his hands around one knee, "I came up here because I just don't like to see you and your mother get into one of these go-rounds, Katie. I know you've got your problems. Being a teenager's a lot tougher than it used to be. But your mother's got hers, too."

"Sure," Katie said. "She just can't forgive me for not bringing her the whole ninth grade to take tango lessons at the studio. How can she be so unrealistic?"

A faint but weary smile played on Katie's father's lips. She noticed for the first time that the whites of his pale eyes were slightly bloodshot and that threadlike mulberry veins colored his cheekbones. "It's not just you, you know," Ralph murmured. "I'm part of the problem, too, Katie."

Katie looked at him with some surprise. "How do you figure that?"

Ralph leaned back again. "Gettin' old, princess." He ran his hand across the thinning top of his sandy hair. "And kind of bald for a hoofer. I don't do the tango very well anymore, either. Your mom's got this vision of the way things were ten, fifteen years ago. She gets mad at me because I keep turning down exhibition dates, especially the ones that pay peanuts — or even less." Ralph sighed. "I'd really like to pull out of the dance business altogether. But I can't tell *her* that."

"Why not?" Katie inquired. "You're doing better in the insurance business now, aren't you? Maybe you *can* close the studio."

Katie's father shook his head. "Got to wait till your mom's ready. Teaching ballroom's her big dream, Katie."

"Some dream," Katie said. "Teaching the cha-cha-cha to a lot of Lloyd Huntzigers. What about you?" She gave her father a searching look. "Don't *you* have a dream?"

Ralph folded his hands behind his head once more. "Yup," he grinned.

Katie hunched forward. "What is it? Tell me."

"It won't thrill you," Ralph promised. "And it wouldn't thrill your mother, either. Which is why I wouldn't dare tell it to her. Yet."

"I'll keep your secret," Katie assured him.

"You'd better," Ralph said with a warning smile. "All I want is to get out of Hooperville for good and do a little fishing off the Florida keys. Now how's that strike you?"

"Terrific," Katie exclaimed. "Do I get to come along?"

Ralph stood up. "Sure. But easy, princess. It all takes time."

Time, Katie thought to herself. Everybody waits too long. Don't they realize you have to sort of *make* things happen?

Ralph dipped his head and aimed a kiss at Katie's cheek. On a sudden impulse, she reached up and threw her arms around his neck.

"Thanks for . . . for coming up to talk to me, Poppa." *Poppa*. She hadn't called her father that since she was eight or nine. She thought Ralph looked a little misty-eyed as he left and softly shut the door behind him.

As soon as her father was gone, Katie dove into the drawer where she kept her diary, dug it out, and opened it to her latest entry. She had begun writing it yesterday, Thursday. But the date above the entry was Saturday — which was tomorrow.

In spite of her awful experience with Rob Garrett, Katie had made up her mind to try again to forecast what she intended to do and then *make* herself go out and do it.

So far, she had written the following:

> *Ninth-grade boys are dumb and there's nobody older in our school. So today I spent the morning over at the mall "shopping around." Looked for any "interesting" possibilities that might come along and even hung around the Take-Your-Own-Photo alcove for a while.*
>
> *After all, I know perfectly well that Tracy Palowski and Kim Brewer don't go to the mall every Saturday just to pick out jeans at Pants 'n More. They go to meet . . . boys.*

Katie sat for a while, crouched over the page, her pen clenched between her teeth. How far should she dare herself to go? Everything she wrote had to become absolutely true by no later than midnight tomorrow. If she made her day vague and general, nothing at all might happen. She had to set herself a real challenge, a goal like meeting somebody who maybe — just maybe — she could take a picture with one of these days when the entry blank for the Romantic Couples Contest arrived in the mail.

Of course, that seemed a lot to hope for. But Katie had to start somewhere. She thought she *had* started when she'd dared herself to talk to Rob Garrett. But after that terrible encounter, she was right back where she had begun.

It still bothered Katie fiercely that Rob Garrett had accused her of being a seventh grader. Sure, Katie was small, although she thought petite was a far nicer word. But she was a lot more than "four feet tall" and she had a figure that definitely came right out and *said* she was fourteen and not eleven or twelve. If Rob hadn't been so busy looking at her braces, he might have seen some of her better points like her eyes, hair, skin, nose, and mouth (although better kept closed, at least until next December).

But the idea of calling her "metalmouth" and then putting his big, dumb, sneakered foot out into the study-hall aisle to try to trip her. . . . He was a juvenile twerp, not worth another moment's thought.

Resolutely, Katie put her pen to the page. Everybody in her family had a dream that was either all wrong or was going to take forever to come true. She felt especially sad about her father. In chasing her own dream of bringing the ballroom back to its glory days, Babette was not only stubbornly hanging on. She was sidetracking Ralph. He'd probably be selling insurance in and around Hooperville until he was eighty to keep paying the losses the failing studio was taking. And those warm, sunny days of fishing off the Florida keys would never happen for him.

Not me, Katie told herself. I'm going to go straight for what I want. I don't expect anybody to help me. But I'm not letting anybody get in my way either. Not Irma, not anybody.

With that, Katie took the plunge. Finishing off her entry for Saturday in bold strokes, she wrote:

Today I met somebody new. And very nice!

She shut the diary with a deliberate air and went back to her Spanish verbs. She was pleasantly surprised to see that the word *amar* was next on her vocabulary list of regular verbs that ended in *ar*.

Amar . . . it meant "to love." Katie sighed. For somebody who was chasing the dream of romance, that might be a very good sign.

CHAPTER
8

Saturday morning was the busiest time of the week at the Hooperville Mall, especially with Easter less than a month away. Although the weather was still raw and blustery and the streets were ridged with humps of grayish ice, the indoor mall was decked with green plants and flowers, both real and artificial. Stuffed bunnies and chicks peered winsomely from the shop windows at the milling crowds. And the overhead lighting felt like warm sun.

The moment Katie got inside and threw off her storm hood, she could feel herself relaxing. This was definitely the right place to be. Even if she ran into Tracy and Kim from school, she wouldn't have to think up an excuse for being here. Although the mall wasn't exactly jumbo-size, you could shop for just about anything from homemade sausage to rock records, from leg-warmers to bikinis. You could make airline reservations to faraway places or get fitted for contact lenses. *And* you could have your photo taken in full color in the privacy of a curtained booth.

This was one of the things Katie intended to do. She wanted to see if she could take a picture that might just make her look like the glamorous half of a "romantic teen couple."

Of course, she realized she was going to need a male partner for the photo she would enter in the Romantic Couples Contest. But, meantime, it wouldn't hurt to take three or four trial photos so she could decide about her hair, the tilt of her head, her expression, and her smile (lips unparted), for when the real thing came along.

After wandering among the crowds and window-shopping for a while, Katie decided to go ahead with the picture-taking. Tossing one last quick look around in case anybody "interesting" came in sight, she veered off into the Take-Your-Own-Photo alcove, ducked into one of the empty booths, and pulled the dark green curtain shut behind her.

There was a mirror on the wall directly above the camera lens. Katie took off her jacket and put her things down on the seat. Then she started arranging her hair, checking her blusher, and carefully applying some apricot lip gloss. She wanted all the colors in the picture to blend with the rich russet highlights of her hair.

Now she began practicing some faces in the mirror, starting by opening her mouth, hanging her tongue out, and letting everything droop as dopily as possible. She'd read in a magazine that this was the way models warmed up to take pictures. Then she began posing. She tried looking like a wholesome, effervescent teen; she tried looking mopey and sultry; she tried looking dreamy and in love; . . . but, of course, it was hard to imagine who with.

Today was the day she was supposed to meet that special someone. Or at least *a* special someone. She'd already told her diary that she *had*. But so far most of the people Katie had seen in her wanderings around the mall were young families on shopping trips — fathers with babies in backpacks, mothers with toddlers in tow.

Maybe it was too early in the day. Tracy and Kim and the boys they came here to meet probably got up later on Saturday mornings. There might not be any "action" until noon at least. But by that time, Katie had to be on her way to the Sunnyside Nursing Home.

Katie watched her expression darken slightly with these discouraging thoughts. Oh well, as long as she was here . . .

She turned from the mirror, settled herself on the little benchlike seat, leveled her head with the camera lens on the wall opposite, dropped her money in the slot, and prepared to smile when the light came on.

It came on a lot faster than Katie had expected it to. She barely had time to get ready. CLICK! That first picture had been awful. She just knew it. Her mouth was *too* scrunched together. Oh, how she hated Rob Garrett for making her more conscious than ever of her braces. *Metalmouth*. Really!

Katie tried to get her lips rearranged for the second shot. She wanted to look pretty and relaxed.

But the warning light startled her. Sure enough, she blinked just as the second CLICK went off. That made her awfully tense. There was no way to stop the camera. It was clicking off too fast.

Katie looked away in desperation and made the droopy, dopey "relaxing" face she'd tried when she'd first entered the booth. She realized that she had been strangely uneasy ever since that moment. Now, she suddenly knew what it was. There was some kind of whispering going on just the other side of the dark green curtain. Listening very, very carefully, Katie could hear breathing, murmuring, even two coughlike bursts of what might have been laughter. The sounds distracted her and the camera went CLICK again before she had a chance to turn around and face it. It had no doubt just taken a picture of the side of her head, probably her right ear.

Katie reached up and snatched at the curtain to pull it closer to the wall. There was a funny kind of a pinch in it that was abruptly released. Could somebody have been holding the curtain just slightly away? Had someone been watching her through the knifelike slit where it hadn't been *quite* closed?

Katie flung the curtain wide open just as the camera clicked off its fourth and final picture. She doubted she was in that one at all.

"Hey!" Katie called out, even though there was nobody in sight. She waited a while, breathing hard. She just knew somebody — probably more than one person — had been standing there a split second earlier.

In response to Katie's shout, a tall, shambling young man wearing an eye shade sauntered over from the change booth in front of the Take-Your-Own-Photo alcove. He sniggered lightly when he saw Katie's outraged face.

"What's up, Sis? Didn't get your pictures yet? Takes four and a half minutes. Gotta read the instructions."

Katie glared up at him. "Somebody was standing out here the whole time, watching me through the side of the curtain. Did you see anybody?"

The young man shook his head. Scrawny hairs grew out of his chin. His nostrils flared and his eyes were cowlike. He could have been sixteen or thirty. He was awful and Katie hoped that *he* wasn't the person she was going to meet today.

"Didn't see nobody," came the reply from under the eye shade. "But then I wasn't lookin'. Not my job."

"At least two of my pictures were ruined," Katie protested. "You'll see when they come out of the slot. I heard whispering and . . . and laughing. And that made me look away."

"No refunds," the young man remarked stubbornly. "You git what you git."

Just then Katie's strip of photos came feeding out of the metal slot like a long, skinny tongue. The young man reached across her into the booth and pulled them out. He looked from the pictures to Katie and back again, his rubbery lips stretching into an elastic grin.

Katie grabbed the pictures away from him. Sure enough the first two were terrible and the last two didn't even have her face on them. Only part of her ear showed on one and the back of her head on the other.

"S'posed to look into the camera," the young man said with amusement. "Too bad. Try again?"

"No thanks," Katie said hotly. She reached for her jacket on the seat of the booth and dashed off with the strip of spoiled photos in her hand. Who could have been spying on her? Was it somebody she knew? Or was it just some kids who hung out at the mall looking for dumb things to do, like watching people who thought that they were all alone trying out silly self-conscious faces for the camera?

Getting her breath back at last, Katie entered a sitting area heady with the smell of hyacinths. A sign said that the live plants were on display by courtesy of the county florists' association and the merchants of the Hooperville Mall. Katie flopped down on one of the benches and waved her strip of photos back and forth to dry them. She had no idea why. Even the first two were hardly worth keeping.

"My, what a heavenly scent."

Katie glanced up. A tall woman with brown hair drawn back into an old-fashioned bun was standing almost directly above her inhaling the fragrance. Beside her, sniffing earnestly, was an all-too-familiar figure.

Katie quickly stuck the photos in her jacket pocket and leaped to her feet. "Irma! What are *you* doing here?"

Irma, half-pleased at seeing Katie, half-alarmed at her challenging tone, looked puzzled for a moment. "This . . . is my mother, Katie. We're shopping." Smiling, Irma held up several parcels in plastic bags. One was actually from the mall's famous unisex jeans store, Pants 'n More.

Katie quickly remembered Irma's second name. "Pleased to meet you, Mrs. DeWitt," she murmured politely.

Irma's mother held out her hand. She had a long, plain face, almost horsey but kind. Her eyes were gray-green. She didn't wear even a trace of makeup.

"Well, I'm happy to meet *you*, Katie. Irma talks about you and your family all the time." Mrs. DeWitt glanced briefly at her daughter and then back to Katie. "In fact, you're the reason we're here today."

Katie gave Irma a questioning look. "Me?" What was this all about?

Irma nodded. "I got *designer* jeans, Katie. A lot like yours. To wear to school. And . . . and other things. Wait till you see how I look next week."

Katie was stunned. She and Irma had never really discussed clothes. But all the time that Katie had been silently observing the way Irma dressed, Irma had probably been trying to get her mother to buy her a new wardrobe to update her appearance. Irma's clothes weren't awful in themselves. They were just different. Katie had no idea Irma had been using her for a sort of model. She was touched by the glow in Irma's eyes as she sank down on the bench and eagerly began to pull something out of one of the parcels.

Mrs. DeWitt smiled half-indulgently. "I guess teens just need to stick together. But Irma never really cared much about dressing like everybody else at school until she met you, Katie."

Katie sat down beside Irma, who was now dragging more purchases out of the packages to show her. "I'm . . . uh . . . really sorry if . . ."

"Oh, don't be," Irma's mother said pleasantly. "It was bound to happen once we moved out of the country and came back to . . . well, 'civilization.' " She leaned down and placed a couple of packages she had been holding on the bench beside Katie and Irma. "Why don't you two chat here for a while? I want to go across to the yarn shop. If I'm not weaving, I like to be knitting. That's just my way."

Katie watched Mrs. DeWitt's departure. "Your mother's nice," she said, turning to Irma. "I didn't know you were so anxious to get a . . . well, different look."

Irma went on holding up tops and T-shirts. She leaned closer. "I even got a new bra. And I'm going to have my hair cut in bangs and let it grow longer. Katie, I'm going to look more like you. Well, not exactly, of course. Because we're not the same type. But you know what I mean."

Katie went on nodding. So this was what Irma's attachment to her had been about, partly anyway. Irma had been studying her. Imitation, Katie had read somewhere, was the sincerest form of flattery. You couldn't be angry at somebody for that. It actually made Katie feel good that Irma had chosen her. It made her feel responsible in a way, too.

Irma began putting things back into their bags. "So this is where you spend your Saturdays, isn't it, Katie?" Irma asked without looking up.

Katie drew back. "Why, no. In fact, I never . . ."

"It's okay," Irma said. "I know a lot of the kids from school hang out around here. Mostly they get together in front of the record shop or around the pizza stand. You probably saw Rob Garrett back there. He was with one of those other boys he's

61

always with in study hall. They were over near that place where you can take your own picture. In those little booths they have. . . ."

Katie's eyes widened in alarm. "Where? Where?"

Irma looked puzzled. "I just told you where. He and this other boy were peeking into one of those booths and laughing hard. I don't know if anybody they knew was in there or not. . . ."

Instantly, the scene that must have taken place outside the photo booth flashed through Katie's mind. Oh, that creep. Rob Garrett had humiliated her again!

"Then," Irma went on, "just as my mother and I were passing the place, they suddenly turned and ran into the crowd. Rob almost tripped me because he ran right in front of me. He didn't see me, though. His face was all red and he was screaming something to the other kid. But I couldn't tell what." Irma paused. "I guess you're still not talking to him, huh?"

Katie thrust her hand nervously into the pocket of her jacket to make sure the strip of photos was still there, hidden from view. So this was what had come of her hopeful morning at the Hooperville Mall. Rob Garrett had spied on her and she hadn't met anybody at all. Except Irma.

Irma was staring persistently at Katie, still waiting for an answer to her question.

"Of *course* I'm not talking to Rob Garrett," Katie told Irma through clenched teeth. "But I *am* sorry I didn't see him." Her eyes flashed fire. "I just *wish* I had."

CHAPTER
9

The warm medicinal air of the Sunnyside Nursing Home wafted soothingly around Katie as she came through the double-door vestibule into the lobby. As usual, a few of the residents sat scattered around, mostly in wheelchairs, watching the comings and goings of visitors. Katie, trying to smile, realized that her face felt stiff and frozen.

It wasn't just her longish trek back here from the mall in the chilling wind. Ever since leaving Irma, with the excuse that she had to get home, Katie had been grimly mulling over in her mind the episode in the photo booth. When, she wondered, had Rob Garrett and his pal started trailing her? How come she'd missed them when she'd looked around just before going into the booth? If they'd been peering through that slit between the curtain and the wall from the very start, they'd have seen her fussing with her hair, putting on her makeup, trying out all those goofy faces in the mirror. . . . Oooh! She was *so* angry.

At the entrance to Jacqui Beamish's office, Katie paused to try to collect herself. She heard her stomach gurgle and realized she hadn't eaten any lunch. She'd grab a snack from the vending machine in the lobby once she was checked in. Or maybe she'd help herself to a container of milk and some Jell-O from the staff lunchroom, as Jacqui often suggested she should.

The door to the activities office stood partly open. It was a small room with Jacqui's desk, some chairs, and a wall of cabinets and open shelves that held the supplies for the arts and crafts program that Jacqui ran at the Sunnyside.

On entering the office, the first thing Katie noticed was that Jacqui's chair was empty. But the room itself wasn't. Somebody — the tallish figure of a young man — was standing at the supply shelves, examining a stuffed toy that one of the residents had probably made.

"Oops," Katie gasped. "I didn't know anybody was in here. Well, I thought Jacqui would be. But I see she isn't."

The person standing at the shelves turned fully to face Katie. Deep-set blue eyes gazed at her out of a strongly masculine face framed with dark bronze curly hair. The toy he was holding was a pudgy bear covered in pink-checked cotton and wearing a kerchief tied under its chin. He held it up and waggled it in front of Katie. His lips worked into a wonderfully mobile smile.

"Grandmother bear," he said in a pleasantly deep voice. "I guess you don't know who made this."

Katie was still trying to come to her senses. She had just turned a corner, her mind on her gurgling stomach and her wasted morning at the mall, and had come face to face with the most attractive boy she had ever seen. He *had* to be sixteen at least. And what in the name of Hooperville High was he doing on a Saturday afternoon in Jacqui Beamish's office at the Sunnyside Nursing Home?

Something like a total meltdown began to take place in the depths of Katie's being. She felt as though her entire body, which had been perfectly solid a moment earlier, was dissolving into a soft, warm ooze. With a tremendous effort at sounding calmly normal, she replied. "No, I don't know. But then I don't work with the patients on crafts projects much. I do . . . um, other things."

"I get it," he said, giving Katie a meaningful look. "You must be the volunteer from Hooperville Middle. Miss Beamish was telling me about you." He placed the stuffed bear back on the shelf. "I'm Chad Hollister. And your name is. . . ."

"Katie," she filled in quickly. She wanted to keep him from saying "Katie Dinkerhoff," just in case Jacqui had told him her last name as well. It would spoil the wonderful moment of their meeting. How could anybody say a word like Dinkerhoff out loud and not start laughing?

Chad Hollister nodded. "Right. Katie. You're the one."

A little thrill ran through Katie's chest. "Oh? The one what?"

Katie sank into a chair. She wondered if she

sounded flirtatious or just plain dumb. She was so dazzled by Chad Hollister and so curious as to why he would know about her that she was ready to accept him no matter what this was all about.

Chad reached for the other chair, turned it around backward, and straddled it facing Katie, his arms dangling over the backrest. "Gee, I'm sorry. I guess nobody had a chance to tell you about me. Miss Beamish got called away to one of the upper floors just after I got here. But she told me to wait for you."

"For me?" Katie asked, still in a dream. "I don't understand."

Chad cleared his throat. He began to talk rapidly. "Yeah, I should explain. Here's the scoop. I'm doing this oral history project over at Hooperville High. It's my sophomore-year field study. That's the reason I'm here. Get it?"

Katie was afraid she didn't get it. She wasn't even sure what oral history was. But how could she let Chad Hollister (high school *sophomore*; *sixteen* for sure; and *gorgeous*) know that? She simply nodded brightly and hoped he'd go on explaining.

"Well, anyway," Chad went on, to Katie's instant relief, "I phoned up here a couple of days ago and asked if I could come over and talk to some of the patients. You know, find out about their earlier lives here in Hooperville, or wherever they come from, farms maybe, places out in the country. This Miss Beamish said she didn't have much time. But there was a girl here who knew the patients and could give me some tips on who to talk to." Chad paused. "That's you, I guess." He grinned a little self-consciously. "Think you can help me?"

Katie was slowly breaking out of her fog. Maybe she did know what Chad Hollister was talking about after all, even if some of his advanced high-school lingo like "oral history" and "field study" had sounded scary and beyond her.

"Oh, I see," she started out slowly, her mind clicking away a lot faster than her tongue. "Well, I guess you might want to talk to somebody like, say . . . Mabel Delacorte."

"Mabel Delacorte?" Chad pounced. "Who's she? Tell me about her." He leaned forward, his eager face nearer to Katie's. She had never in her life met a boy who was close to her own age, yet had such an unusual interest. There were lots of boys who were totally wrapped up in sports or science fiction or pop music. But oral history? Collecting the life stories of people old enough to be their great-grand-parents?

"Well," Katie said thoughtfully, "I don't think she's from a farm. I think she's always been a town person. . . ."

Chad nodded. "That's okay. How old is she?"

Katie found herself looking directly into Chad's eyes. Their blueness was startling but she willed herself not to blink. "Ninety-two maybe. She's in a wheelchair. But you've got to see the way she has her hair fixed by a beautician every week. And the way she makes up her face. Most of the time, she likes me to read her these romance novels. . . ."

Rapid footsteps, punctuated with sneezes, were approaching along the corridor. Katie stopped herself and looked up. Chad followed her gaze.

"Ahh," Jacqui Beamish's heavy voice boomed as she entered the room, "here you are. I see you two found each other. Good."

Chad had risen from his chair on seeing Jacqui and now Katie did the same. She wondered if Jacqui had any idea how truly "good" it was that she and Chad had "found each other."

"Chad's told you, I guess, about his project," Jacqui said to Katie, as she whipped out a handkerchief and began blowing her nose. She seemed to have a fresh case of the sniffles.

"Um-hmmm," Katie replied. "I thought I'd introduce him first to Mrs. Delacorte. She might have an interesting life story. And she always says she's 'holding on to the dream.' I keep wondering what dream that is."

Jacqui, leafing through some papers on her desk, looked up. "Good idea." She shifted her glance to Chad. "Mabel Delacorte's one of our more glamorous patients. Her health's rather frail though, so go easy, you understand." Jacqui paused, her dark eyes twinkling. "Of course *you* won't have any trouble with her. She'll go for you head over heels."

Chad actually looked embarrassed. Didn't he *know* how good-looking he was?

A few moments later, he and Katie started down the corridor together. She couldn't believe she was walking next to the "somebody new. And *very* nice!" that she had recklessly promised herself in her diary entry for today. How had this happened? Was there an all-seeing, all-knowing "romance" spirit out there that had finally decided to bestow on Katie the makings of her dream?

Of course not. Katie didn't believe in the supernatural. She had started to write the next day's events in her diary only for the purpose of forcing herself to be bolder, to take some risks, so that the world around her and its opportunities wouldn't pass her by easily. She had never counted on the miraculous coincidence of a Chad Hollister appearing out of the blue. *And* at the Sunnyside Nursing Home, a place so lacking in romantic possibilities, Katie had thought, that she had never even mentioned it in her diary.

Now that Chad Hollister *had* come on the scene, though, Katie was certainly not going to let go of him easily, in the pages of her diary *or* anywhere else. If he only knew what designs she had on him. She shuddered and blushed at the same moment, thinking of how her next step would be to figure out a way of getting a photo of Chad and herself for the Romantic Couples Contest.

Katie turned to look at him, as if testing the reality. She hoped he didn't think she was too short for him. She definitely didn't think *he* was too tall for her. "Um," she suggested, "we have a few minutes before Mrs. Delacorte comes down from her room. Would you like a . . . a Coke or something?" They were approaching the vending machine in the lobby and Katie's stomach was threatening a brand new barrage of burbles and gurgles.

Chad stopped and hastily thrust his hand in his pocket. She could hear some change rattling. "No. But I'd like to buy you one. For helping me out. I'd never get to poke around here without someone they already know and trust."

Katie shook her head vehemently. "Oh no. I couldn't let you. Anyhow, I have a better idea. Why don't we both go get some milk from the staff lunchroom? It's over this way."

A few minutes later they were sitting across from each other at one of the empty tables. Chad was drinking his milk from the container. Katie was sipping hers through a straw and delicately spooning up Jell-O from a small dish on the side. She had suddenly become terribly conscious of her braces, and she was afraid to speak. Could she ever forget the carrot shred dangling from her teeth that had been the beginning of all her troubles with Rob Garrett?

Katie's silence must have been catching, because Chad seemed to have lost his tongue, too. What if they never thought of another thing to say to each other? Katie looked up, their eyes met, and Chad coughed a few times.

"So . . . um, there's this dream that, ah, Mabel Delacorte is holding on to," he said, trying to get the conversation going again.

Katie gulped and a glob of Jell-O slid noiselessly down her throat. "Yes," she said with relief. "I think everybody ought to have some kind of dream, don't you?"

Chad Hollister nodded. Was he serious or was he just trying to be agreeable?

"It's important," Katie added, defending her position. "Do you have one?"

Chad hunched one shoulder. "Sure, I guess so."

Katie wondered if she would ever have the nerve to ask him to tell her his dream. If she did ask him, she'd have to be prepared to tell him hers, wouldn't she?

Suppose Chad asked her to tell him *her* dream

this very minute. Katie caught her breath. She suddenly had this zany vision of herself, sitting there, looking directly into Chad's eyes, and forming the words, "My dream . . . is you."

But of course she didn't do any such thing. "We . . . we ought to be going," Katie stammered.

As she crumpled her milk carton and started to push back her chair, she thought Chad looked at her strangely. Had he read her mind? Did he think she was weird? Would Katie ever be able to behave like a normal person in Chad Hollister's presence?

CHAPTER
10

"Katie, telephone," Aunt Zoe called out. "It's that boy again."

Katie leaped off the studio bed in her room and sliced her way through a heap of school books and homework papers that lay scattered on the rug. Today was Friday and, what was even more important, tomorrow was Saturday. It was the second time this week that Chad Hollister had phoned, and the sound of his voice so close to her ear had sent thrilling vibrations through Katie's entire being.

The telephone was in a dark alcove at the top of the stairs, near Katie's room. But she wished she had a private line in her own room. She hated the idea that any member of the family might overhear her conversation with Chad.

Zoe was waiting down at the bottom of the stairs for Katie to pick up.

"Heartthrob, huh?" Zoe hissed as Katie rushed past the upstairs landing and waved Zoe away. She knew she wouldn't be comfortable until she heard Zoe hang up the downstairs extension.

"Hi," Katie breathed into the phone in a half-whisper.

"Katie, this is Chad. I'm sorry to bother you."

Click went the downstairs receiver, back onto its cradle. Katie didn't mind Chad's sounding businesslike when Aunt Zoe might have been listening. But he'd sounded that way all *through* their last conversation. Katie wished he would relax more.

"Oh . . . ah, no bother," Katie said, relieved to know she was truly alone now with Chad. "How are you?"

"Oh fine, fine. Just calling to tell you I . . . uh, found I could make it over to the Sunnyside tomorrow, after all. Will you be there?"

"Of course, Chad," Katie replied, trying to hide her eagerness. "I'm always there on Saturdays."

"Great," he said. "My adviser really liked the stuff I did so far on Mrs. Delacorte. Do you think you could introduce me to anyone else? Maybe a man this time?"

"A man?" Katie remarked. She had thought of Mrs. Handelsmann, a stout lady with chin whiskers who had been born in Germany and still liked to talk about "the old days when the kaiser ruled" to anyone who would listen. Katie figured Mrs. Handelsmann, with her throaty foreign accent, would be an interesting contrast to Mabel Delacorte who was a fourth-generation American.

"Any problem with finding me a man?" Chad asked after Katie took some time answering.

"No, I guess not," Katie said. "Of course there's only about one man to every ten women over at the Sunnyside. Women live a lot longer than men, you know."

"Yup," Chad replied quietly. "Guess that's true."

A terrible image suddenly hit Katie hard. She could just see Chad Hollister dying — about seventy years from now — and leaving her absolutely flat. She knew she was being ridiculous. She didn't even know if Chad liked her, let alone whether she'd still know him when he was eighty-six! With an effort, Katie jolted herself back to the present, which was uncertain enough.

"There *is* one man," Katie began. "He has this scrapbook full of newspaper clippings. They're all 'letters to the editor' that he used to write that got printed — "

"Good," Chad said almost abruptly. "Sounds fine." His voice dropped to a slightly more personal level. "And I'll see you tomorrow, Katie. Around one? Like last week?"

"Like last week," Katie echoed softly. Then she put the phone down and started to tiptoe blissfully back to her room. The conversation hadn't ever gotten past being "strictly business," but to Katie it felt like they had just made a romantic date.

She hadn't yet reached her door, when she heard Zoe calling from downstairs. "Katie, are you off?"

Katie leaned over the bannister. "You know I'm off. You've been listening the whole time. So why are you asking?"

Zoe was standing at the bottom of the stairs hold-

74

ing something that looked like a postcard in her hand.

"Katie, I wasn't. I swear it. Your first heavy boyfriend. Would I do a thing like that? Don't get mad. I'm coming up."

Katie watched Zoe's slight figure rapidly mount the dark, polished wood steps. Her big round glasses always seemed to glint more when she was slightly agitated.

"Here," she said, partly out of breath. "I was waiting to give you this when nobody else was around. They're both in the studio now with the Friday night Latin dance rhythms group. It came in the late-afternoon mail and I put it aside for you." Zoe thrust the post card into Katie's hand. " 'K.T. Dinkerhoff,' it says. That *is* you, isn't it?"

Katie stared down at the card on which her name was printed in businesslike type. The return address consisted of the initials *RCC* and a box number. She knew in a split second what it was. Katie turned the card over and rapidly scanned the printed message:

> Thank you for your interest in entering our *Romantic Couples Contest*. You will soon be receiving an official entry blank. Your submission will be given every consideration in keeping with the contest rules. We wish you the best of luck!

Katie flipped the card back to the address side. "You read it, didn't you?" she said to Zoe.

Zoe flung an arm around Katie's shoulders and began marching her slowly toward her room. "Nobody puts a private message on a postcard, honeysuckle. Anyhow, I wasn't even sure who it was for. What's with this 'K.T. Dinkerhoff' business?"

Katie dipped her head. "I . . . um . . . just sort of made it up. I figured it would get more . . . respect."

Zoe looked surprised. "You mean you actually sent away to be in this contest?"

"Yes," Katie said defiantly. "Anything wrong with that?" Zoe was a fine one to talk after all the weird schemes she'd tried out.

They had reached the doorway of Katie's room and were awkwardly trying to decide who should go through it first. Katie finally went in ahead and flopped down on the bed.

Zoe remained in the doorway. She hunched her shoulders. "Well, the chance of winning is so. . . ." She stopped herself. "Oh, I get it. It's this new boyfriend. Is he as gorgeous as that voice of his? How did you meet him?" Zoe advanced into the room, leaned over, and cupped Katie's chin in her hand. "Oh, you're a sly one, Miss K.T. Dinkerhoff. Never a peep out of you. Does your mother know? Of course not. You and she are still fighting the cold war over whether Irma takes waltz lessons or not."

"Listen," Katie said, leaning back and hugging a pillow in her arms, "you've got it all wrong. About Chad, about the contest. I wrote away a long time ago. Before I ever met him. That only happened last Saturday at the Sunnyside Nursing Home. But I wanted it all to be a secret."

"Secrets," Zoe said, bouncing down beside Katie. "You know I'll keep your secrets. Haven't I always? Why do you think I waited till the coast was clear to give you your mail? When it comes to romance, or anything else, you can always confide in your old Aunt Zoe." Zoe straightened up and folded her arms across her chest. "Because even though I may not look it, I've gone that whole romance route, baby. And I don't mean with some tame widower like Lloyd Huntziger either."

Katie smiled. She supposed she needed somebody in the Dinkerhoff household she could trust. For one thing, there'd be more mail coming from the contest people. So she told Zoe about how she'd accidentally found the contest announcement in Mabel Delacorte's paperback book, the rules about sending in the photo and the fifty-word essay on being a couple, and the first-prize romantic weekend in New York City.

Zoe smacked her lips together. "And now you've even got the guy. See, it *is* possible to make things happen. Didn't I always say, 'You gotta have a dream?'"

Katie examined her cuticles critically. She hadn't told Zoe about her diary entries, about writing down the things she hoped would happen to her *in advance*, as a means of trying to get her dreams to come true. Some things were just too personal.

"I haven't 'got' him yet," Katie reminded Zoe. "I need to have him take a picture with me. How am I going to do that? Lots of boys are camera shy when it comes to taking a photo with a girl. They never know what she's going to do with it."

Zoe giggled. "How right they are. Suppose you got the picture and you sent it in and you won. Do you think he'd go to New York with you?"

Katie shuddered slightly. "One step at a time. Isn't that what you always say?"

Zoe grabbed Katie's hands and squeezed them hard between hers. "That's my girl. I'm real proud of you, doll." She squeezed even harder, making Katie wince. "And I'm rooting for you all the way. Remember that."

After Zoe left, Katie went into her itchy-sweater drawer and fished out her diary. She hadn't written anything in it since last Friday, when she had boldly added to the page headed *Saturday*:

> *Today I met somebody new. And very nice!*

And that had come true. Now Katie had to forecast something wonderful for tomorrow. Did she dare hope for a picture with Chad for when the official entry form for the Romantic Couples Contest arrived?

Wistfully, Katie let her pen touch the blank page. Maybe there really was a fairy godmotherlike "romance" spirit who would mysteriously guide her hand when the words began to flow.

Katie took a deep breath and watched herself write:

> *His name is Chad Hollister and he's very special. He telephoned me twice this week.*
>
> *Today, Saturday, I saw him again at the Sunnyside Nursing Home where we first met. And we had a picture taken — together!*

CHAPTER
11

Early on Saturday morning, Irma phoned Katie. "Did I wake you up?" Irma inquired.

Actually Katie had been too nervous to sleep very well. Today was the big day, the day of the "impossible dream," the day for getting a photo of Chad and herself for the Romantic Couples Contest.

Katie had emerged from the bathroom on the second ring hoping it was Chad and, at the same time, hoping it wasn't. Suppose he was phoning to say he couldn't make it today after all? She'd have gone right back in the bathroom and drowned herself.

So in a way Katie was rather relieved to hear Irma's voice.

"No, I'm up," she told Irma. "But why are you calling so early?"

"I know it's early," Irma said, "but I wondered if you were going to the mall today. See, there's one thing I got there last week that I have to exchange. And also I need some more socks. And I figured if you were going anyway, I could come over to your house and we could go together. . . ."

"But Irma," Katie interrupted gently, "I already told you, I don't go to the mall on Saturdays. Last week was an exception, purely a . . . an accident."

Irma seemed not to hear. "Katie, I'll be wearing some of the stuff I got last week. You liked the things I wore to school. You said designer jeans were really my style."

It was true that Irma had gotten herself a whole new look and her nerdlike image around school was fading fast. Katie had been feeling pleased that Irma was so much happier about herself. She had a really impressive figure in her new clothes — long legs, much better posture, and a very nice chest. Kids had actually turned to admire her in school, and a couple of girls had asked her where she'd bought some of her things.

Katie had had a pretty good week at school, too. She'd been buoyed up by her delicious new secret, otherwise known as Chad Hollister. And her expected confrontation with Rob Garrett never materialized. Maybe it was the genuine "drop dead" look that Katie had given him on Monday as she and Irma were entering study hall. Maybe Rob *had* seen Irma passing the Take-Your-Own-Photo alcove after all and figured that she'd told Katie about his spying on her. Anyhow, he'd slunk around school the rest of the week like a dog with its tail between its legs and generally made his presence scarce. Katie was perfectly pleased. She considered him beneath contempt.

"Irma," Katie said apologetically into the phone, "I'd honestly go with you if I could. But I have something else to do today. What about your mother? Can't she go?"

There was a pause. Katie almost thought the line had gone dead. Finally Irma's voice came back on. "It's not the same, Katie. I could go all by myself, too, you know. I just wanted somebody I could . . . well, hang out with. We could go later in the day, whenever you say. Have lunch or a snack there. . . ."

Katie was really uncomfortable. She was truly sorry she couldn't go to the mall with Irma. But she was awfully tense about what she had written in her diary for today. It was hard to concentrate on anything but Chad. She promised herself she'd make it all up to Irma real soon. It was time to stop having all these secrets from her. It was unfair to Irma and was getting to be a real burden for Katie.

"I could go with you tomorrow, Irma," Katie suggested hopefully. "We'd have the whole day together. How about that?"

"I can't make it tomorrow," Irma replied. "And anyhow I have to return that top that's too tight today. It's a seven-day exchange. They won't take it back tomorrow because that's the eighth day."

Katie sighed. "Well, then . . . I guess I'll see you in school on Monday."

"I guess so," Irma mumbled. There was a funny, gulping noise on the word "so." Katie hoped that

Irma wasn't choking back tears or anything like that. Katie felt bad enough as it was.

The door to Katie's parent's room closed softly down the hall and Babette appeared. She was wrapped in a heavy white chenille bathrobe with strands of gold thread in it and she looked tousled from sleep.

"Morning, Katie," Babette yawned. "Who was that on the phone so early?"

Katie flinched. She hoped Babette wasn't about to revive last week's argument about her bringing Irma to the nursing home with her. It was bad enough that Katie was feeling so awful right now about Irma.

Babette put her head coquettishly to one side. "Maybe that was too personal a question. I'm still half asleep, honey, so don't mind me."

Katie steeled herself. "That was Irma on the phone," she replied. "But . . . um, she and I couldn't get together today. I guess it's too early in the morning for you and me to have a fight about that."

Babette, who had started for the bathroom, turned and gave Katie a concerned look. "Listen, Katie, honey, I don't want to fight with you ever. I feel bad about last week. I feel bad that we haven't been . . . getting along. I'm always so worried about that darned studio. I get crazy sometimes. I want people to care about it the way I do. And they won't."

Katie sensed that her mother was talking about her father as well as herself. Babette reached up and fluffed her hair. "Let me get washed up," she suggested, "and I'll come downstairs and make you some breakfast. Just the two of us, huh? Something unhealthy that Zoe would disapprove of. Like bacon, sausage, fried eggs, hash-brown potatoes." Babette giggled.

Katie looked doubtful. She knew she wouldn't be able to eat much breakfast with her stomach fluttering the way it was today. But then she was pretty sure Babette wasn't serious about cooking all those things, either. Zoe did most of the food shopping and there surely wasn't any bacon or sausage in the house.

About ten minutes later, Katie and her mother were downstairs, seated at the breakfast table having toasted English muffins and juice.

"The Latin dance rhythms group has shrunk to *three* students," Babette remarked, buttering a muffin and shaking her head. "The Kibbees couldn't make it last night. He has circulatory problems in his legs and she threw her back out square dancing. That means they'll probably drop away for good. Oh, what should I do, Katie? I'm just not ready to give up the studio. I want five more years. Is that too much to ask?"

Katie looked away uncomfortably. Was this going to be the beginning of another drive to recruit Katie's classmates to ballroom dancing?

Babette must have read Katie's thoughts. She reached across the table and patted her hand reassuringly. "Okay, okay. I know I sound like a broken record. Most of Hooperville is dying of old age and I should start teaching aerobics or something else that younger people want."

Babette got up to pour herself some coffee. "But, honey, there's just no romance in all that jumping around and perspiring. No glamour, no beauty." Babette returned to the table. "Still, I'll have to think

83

of something. Your father's anxious to get out, too, so I won't even have a dance partner. He doesn't say much, but I can sense it."

Katie hunched her shoulders. "I don't know what to say. I guess times change, that's all. You should probably get yourself a new dream. But I don't know what."

Babette set her coffee cup down and rested her chin in her hand. "A new dream," she mused. "You're so funny, Katie. But you're right. If I could just get down to New York City for a while, look up some of my old contacts, make some new ones. I still think I could put together an exhibition tour. Half a dozen U.S. cities. Maybe Canada. There's still plenty of interest in seeing ballroom beautifully staged and performed. But it has to start where the action is. Not here."

Katie leaned back and looked at her mother with satisfaction. "See, you're getting some ideas already. Now just start putting it all down step by step and . . . and *make* it happen!"

But Babette had slumped back in her chair like a deflating balloon. "Ahh, that's all it is. A dream. I'm a has-been who's had it, honey. Let's not talk about me. Tell me about you. What are your plans for today?"

Katie wondered if her mother was getting a little absent-minded. "I'm going to the nursing home. Remember? It's Saturday."

Babette shook her head. "Oh, that's right. I sometimes think I'm getting ready for a room at the Sunnyside myself. Do you find it depressing going there, Katie? I'd figured that at your age it wouldn't seem too sad."

"No," Katie said. "It's really okay. It even gets . . . interesting at times." She was half-tempted to tell her mother about Chad, but quickly dropped the idea. It was enough — probably too much — that Zoe knew her secret. "Well," Katie went on, "I mean, take someone like Mabel Delacorte who keeps up her looks and is so. . . ." A sudden thought struck Katie. "You know what? I'd love to take a picture of Mrs. Delacorte. Do you still have that Polaroid camera that you use for taking photos in the studio?"

Babette rubbed her temple. "Of course. Though I don't think we've taken a single picture since the Christmas ball. Now that was rather a success. I wonder what would happen if we planned an open-house spring cotillion. I must talk to — "

"Could I borrow it?" Katie asked, leaning forward eagerly.

Babette was off on one of her schemes again. "What?"

"Borrow it?" Katie repeated. "The camera. Just for the afternoon. I'll take good care of it. Mrs. Delacorte would really love having a photo of herself. Maybe I'll snap some of the other patients, too."

"Oh sure, I guess so," Babette said. "Something to make the dear old souls feel a bit happier. Why not?"

Later that morning, walking through streets spangled with early spring sunshine, the camera in her shoulder bag, Katie was still congratulating herself on her brain wave.

She knew that Jacqui Beamish had a camera for

taking instant pictures of the patients during special events at the nursing home. There was even a bulletin board outside the arts and crafts room with a selection of recent photos taken at one of the monthly birthday parties.

Katie had hoped to borrow that camera to somehow get a photo of Chad and herself. But she had been a long way from figuring out what her reason would be. She *still* had no idea how she would maneuver the picture-taking. She only knew that what she had written down in her diary for today *had* to come true, and that she was now a lot closer to her goal.

The long, gray stone building of the Sunnyside Nursing Home came into view as Katie rounded the corner of Cavendish Avenue. It seemed to her that the broad, straw-colored lawn that fronted the building and sloped away toward the street was showing the faintest sign of greening. Spring was actually on its way, and her secret plans were going well. Everything was in place.

In fact, Chad Hollister might already be inside the building — waiting. He had given Katie his word that he would be there. Surely nothing could happen to disappoint her now.

CHAPTER
12

As Katie pulled open the heavy front door of the Sunnyside Nursing Home, she was bewildered by the sound of giggling. It was coming from the enclosed entry passage, just inside the doorway, that was designed to keep cold drafts from drifting directly into the lobby. Stepping into the passage, Katie found herself even more baffled.

A teenage girl was sitting on the tiled vestibule floor, her head bent and her shoulders shaking with laughter. Standing above her, leaning against the wall, was a second girl. She was trying to smother her giggles, without much success.

A curtain of silky blonde hair hid the face of the girl seated on the floor. But one glance at the girl who was standing told Katie all she needed to know. Shocked, Katie found herself looking directly into the slightly narrowed eyes of Tracy Palowski. The girl on the floor had to be her blonde lookalike and best friend, Kim Brewer.

"Kim," Tracy urged in a hurried, slightly sobered whisper as soon as she saw Katie, "get up! There's somebody here. Somebody I think you know." Tracy warily shifted her attention back to Katie. "*This* is a surprise. What are *you* doing here?"

Katie drew herself up to her full height. She was still a couple of inches shorter than Tracy, the taller of the two attractive and popular ninth graders.

"I could ask you the same question," Katie re-marked. She stared down at Kim, who had raised her head and was looking up at Katie with a puzzled expression.

"Who-o-o?" Kim asked, still limp with laughter. "Who's that?"

Tracy bent over, grabbed Kim's arm, and yanked her to her feet. "Maybe you can tell better from up here, featherbrain," she said with a grin. She shook Kim by the shoulder. "Recognize her now?"

"Oh yeah," Kim said slowly, when she saw Katie. She rubbed her arm where Tracy had pulled at it. "I've seen you in the lunchroom lots of times. With that friend of yours. The one who looks like a . . . Raggedy Ann doll." Kim glanced slyly at Tracy. "I guess it's that haircut. Mostly."

"Irma," Katie said in a stony voice, taking Irma's side at once. "Her name is Irma. And in case you don't know mine," she glanced from Kim to Tracy, "I'm Katie. You still didn't say what the two of you are doing here."

Tracy dug her thumbs into the loops of her pants belt and gave Katie a gunslinger look. "Neither did you." Apparently Tracy wasn't going to bother introducing Kim or herself. She probably just assumed that everybody in school knew who *they* were.

Tracy tossed her head defiantly and Katie noticed that her long, straight, blonde hair was thicker than Kim's and had darker streaks in it. But both girls were snub-nosed and pretty in a teen movie-star kind of way. Kim had the rounder face, Tracy had the stronger features. They still could have passed for sisters.

"I work here," Katie said, preparing to cut the talk and shoulder her way past them, "and I'm almost late."

"Ooh, you don't say." It was Kim's voice. She suddenly seemed impressed by Katie. "Are you a volunteer?"

Katie felt a swooning sensation in the pit of her stomach. She had a horrible foreboding that she knew what was coming next. She nodded weakly. "Yes."

"So are we!" Tracy and Kim replied in unison. They laughed and linked the pinkies of their right hands in some secret ritual.

"Now we can all three go in together," Tracy said almost chummily to Katie. "See, we got here early and we didn't know what we should do. And birdbrain, here" — she glanced at Kim and tugged at her friend's sweater — "got cold feet and started giggling. She didn't want to come in the first place because she says old people give her the creeps. Did you ever see that horror movie where time speeds up and everybody gets real old in about — "

Kim poked at Tracy's shoulder in protest. "Well, it wasn't my idea. You dragged me here. I'd have been over at the high-school stadium today watching spring practice if it wasn't for you. It's too nice a day to be indoors anyway."

Tracy made a mock-threatening fist at Kim and lightly shoved her backward. "Don't listen to her," she told Katie. "She's such a fruitcake."

Katie frowned, wishing they would both instantly disappear and she could escape into the lobby. Already some of the patients were peering through the glass into the vestibule, wondering at the antics of the three girls who stood there talking and gesturing.

"My Aunt Louise works here," Tracy explained. "She's a physical therapist. Only she's not here on Saturdays. She came over to our house last week and told my mother they need teenage volunteers. My mother said Kim and I should do some sensible thing like that instead of clowning around and chasing boys all the time."

Kim giggled accusingly at Tracy. "*You* chase boys."

Tracy gave her a half-angry look. "*You* drool all over them. You don't even give them a fighting chance." She turned to Katie. "She's like one of those flowers with the sticky goo all over them," Tracy waggled her fingers, "that swallow whatever insect happens to fly anywhere near them. Know the kind I'm talking about?"

Katie nodded helplessly.

"Anyhow," Tracy went on, linking her arm through Katie's and indicating for Kim to attach herself to Katie's other arm, "we're here and we're supposed to see this lady who's in charge of recreation. Miss Beamish?" She chuckled. "Is that really her name? Are you supposed to see her, too?"

Before Katie could answer, Tracy had pushed open the vestibule door and charged into the lobby. Mrs. Handelsmann, the wheelchair-bound German lady, who happened to be sitting near the entrance, gave Katie a nod accompanied by a surprised stare.

Neither Tracy nor Kim took any notice. Nor did they see the sickly smile Katie managed to give Mrs. Handelsmann as she passed her. For by that time Katie had broken ranks with the two girls and was grimly leading the way to Jacqui Beamish's office, where Chad Hollister might very well be waiting for her.

Half an hour later, Katie was breathing easier but only a *tiny* bit. Chad, fortunately, had been late and the three girls found only Jacqui waiting for them in the corridor outside the crafts room next door to her office.

"Tracy and Kim, Kim and Tracy," Jacqui said, ushering them into the crafts room and handing them stiff paper badges and a couple of colored felt-tip markers. "I'll never tell you apart. But even more important, the patients have to know who you are. Write your names, *big*, and underneath write 'volunteer.' It's a house rule. You have to pin them on before you go on duty."

Tracy looked up from the letters she was printing on her badge in bright grassy green. "What about her?" She pointed her marker at Katie.

Katie had carefully put her shoulder bag with Babette's camera in it down on one of the work tables. She was just slipping off her jacket. Her badge, with her name drawn on it in passion pink, was already pinned to her shirt.

Jacqui waved her hand. "Oh, Katie's an old-timer here. She already has one."

Kim, standing bent-over beside Tracy, filling in her own badge, thrust out her lip in a pout. "Oh, she didn't tell us that."

"You didn't ask me," Katie said, keeping her voice as steady as she could. Her eyes remained fixed on the open doorway. Suppose Chad arrived this very minute. Would he go directly into Jacqui's office or, hearing voices next door, head for the crafts room? Was there any way in the world that Katie could keep Chad from crossing paths with Tracy and Kim? The Sunnyside Nursing Home wasn't big enough. All of Hooperville wasn't big enough. Sooner or later they'd find him and they'd try to take him away from her — Chad, her beautiful secret. His very existence, Katie felt, was something she had dreamed up and made into a reality . . . through sheer force of will.

Happily, Jacqui took Tracy and Kim away with her about five minutes later for an "orientation" tour of the Home. Katie was supposed to make "floor" visits to a short list of patients who were her regulars and then help wheel them to the main lounge for the afternoon's activity, which today was a game called "horse racing."

Jacqui gave Katie a last look over her shoulder. "See you later then. Around two." If Jacqui knew Chad was coming today, she didn't say anything to Katie about it. And Katie certainly had no intention of mentioning his name while Tracy and Kim were within hearing.

As soon as they left, Katie had gone into Jacqui's office to wait for Chad. It was about a quarter past one. Nervously, Katie kept peering out into the corridor. If Jacqui came back, she'd want to know why Katie hadn't started her rounds.

When Katie saw him at last, she beckoned him into the office urgently. "What's up, Katie?" he asked, pulling his arms out of his jacket as he approached. "You . . . look worried."

She realized how tense she'd been and broke into a sheepish smile. "It's nothing. Only I was supposed to start visiting some of my patients and I was waiting for you."

Chad hung his jacket on the rack in Jacqui's office next to Katie's. Tracy and Kim had left theirs in the wardrobe in the crafts room. Chad glanced at his watch. "Sorry I'm late." He was carrying a large leatherlike portfolio that zipped up around the edges. "Let's get started," Chad said. He sounded hurried and matter-of-fact. Katie told herself it was partly her fault.

As they went toward the elevator together, Chad patted the portfolio under his arm. "Brought all my stuff along this week," he said. "Got a new tape recorder, too."

The elevator was empty. As they got in, Chad accidentally brushed against Katie. He continued to stand close to her, and she felt herself starting to blush as she pushed the button for the third floor. That was where Chad would be able to meet the man with all the newspaper clippings whom he hoped to interview next. Katie wasn't sure where Jacqui had taken Tracy and Kim. She just hoped the topmost floor would be safe from them.

"So, um, how've you been, Katie?" Chad asked, after the elevator door closed. He was different now.

There was warmth in his voice, as his eyes searched hers. If Chad acted this way all the time, Katie figured she'd die.

Oh, she thought, forgetting to breathe. I love him. I love him more than ever.

"I've been . . . uh . . . wonderful," she answered. She hoped that didn't sound conceited. She hadn't meant it that way.

When the elevator door opened at three, they were still standing close to each other. Katie wished they could have stayed there, slowly going from floor to floor in a building as tall as one of the towers in New York City — one of the very buildings in which she might some day find herself with Chad if her dream about the Romantic Couples Contest came true.

I won't let anybody take him away from me, Katie vowed fiercely to herself. I'll kill before I'll let either of those two boy-crazy creeps . . . get their paws on him!

CHAPTER
13

Mabel Delacorte leaned to one side of her wheelchair and whispered to Katie, "Where's your fella today, darling?"

Katie had just come down to the main lounge to set up the "horses" — actually a row of six numbered wooden horseheads for the nickel-a-chance betting game that the Sunnyside residents liked to play. Chad was still safely tucked away on the third floor talking to Mr. Elwood, the proud author of over two hundred published "letters to the editor."

"Oh, Chad's here," Katie assured her, "and he wants to see you later this afternoon for a few more notes on your . . . life story."

Mrs. Delacorte chuckled delightedly. "Anything. Anytime. You tell him, my dear, I'll be ready. He's the perfect Mr. Romance Hero, don't you think?

Oh, if any of my leading men had ever looked like him. I wouldn't have needed to work so hard at my acting in the love scenes."

It had turned out that Mabel Delacorte had once been the star of a traveling repertory company that performed operettas and musical comedies. She had allowed Chad to look through the scrapbooks that she kept locked away in her room. Although she had been secretive for years with the people at the Sunnyside, she had opened her life to him after only a few minutes of talk.

Katie nodded. She couldn't have agreed more with what Mabel Delacorte had said about Chad being the perfect Mr. Romance Hero. In Katie's eyes, he could have sprung, dressed in the right period costume, out of the pages of any of the romance novels that Katie had read to Mrs. Delacorte.

"By the way," Katie said, "I have a camera with me today. When Chad comes down to talk to you, I'd like to take a picture of you. If you'll let me."

"Oh," Mrs. Delacorte fluttered, "you can bet on it." She leaned forward. "Even better, dearie. You can take a picture of him and me together."

"I'll be glad to," Katie replied. Chad surely wouldn't object. He'd probably want the photo for his oral history files. *And* it would give Katie a chance to have a photo of him.

But, leaving Mrs. Delacorte's side, Katie was still wondering *who* was going to take a picture of Chad and herself. Could she possibly trust the veiny, trembling hands and failing eyesight of Mrs. Delacorte? Would Chad think it an odd request on Katie's part? Was it too forward? And how was she going to carry the whole thing off away from the prying eyes of Tracy and Kim?

The main lounge was beginning to fill up for the afternoon's activity. As Katie had expected, Jacqui had put Tracy and Kim to work wheeling patients into the room and arranging their chairs in a convenient circle. Jacqui herself was getting ready to start the horse-racing game. She would toss a pair of dice. Then, according to the numbers that showed up, the horses would be moved forward, bit by bit, toward the finish line.

Kim, slightly flushed, sidled up to Katie. "I never realized how much work this was going to be. I mean, getting all those wheelchairs in and out of the elevator, we just about had a case of gridlock. Tracy and I were up on the second floor. Where've *you* been all this time?"

"Third," Katie murmured.

"What's up there?" Kim asked almost suspiciously.

"Oh, just more of the same," Katie replied, trying to sound casual. "I made visits to some of the patients I know pretty well. And then I brought them down here, just like you and Tracy did."

"How long have you been coming here anyway?" Kim wanted to know.

"A few months," Katie mumbled, busying herself with repositioning some of the chairs so the patients in them would have a better view of the "race track."

Kim followed close behind Katie. "And what about your friend, the one you eat lunch with?"

Katie looked up. "You mean Irma. What about her?"

Kim shrugged. "Well . . . um, Tracy and I were wondering. How come she isn't a volunteer, too?"

Katie put another wheelchair into a better position. "We don't do everything together. Irma had someplace else she had to go today." But, secretly, Katie found herself wishing Irma were here. Was it too late, she wondered, to confess about Saturdays and ask Irma to join her?

"Hmmm," Kim remarked. "Tracy and I are practically like one person." She looked across the room to where Tracy was helping a patient with a walker to settle herself at one end of a long sofa. Kim waved her fingers almost flirtatiously at her friend. "We agree on almost everything," Kim went on. "Like we told you, I didn't want to come here with Tracy today. But I came. The only thing we ever . . . fight about . . . is . . . boys."

Kim's speech had become slower and slower. On the word *boys*, Katie heard a gasp, and then silence. She glanced at Kim, followed the direction of her gaze, saw what Kim had just seen, and knew at once what had happened. Chad had just appeared in the doorway of the main lounge!

Kim, standing alongside Katie, was already on her toes, making frantic gestures to Tracy to try to direct her attention to Chad's tall, handsome figure. The very next moment, Chad spotted Katie and began making his way toward her.

All too soon, he was at Katie's side. Katie had never been so sorry to see him. She had known from the start that there wasn't a chance she'd be able to keep him away from Tracy and Kim for the entire afternoon. But she had hoped against hope for some magical barrier that would shield him from their view. Instead, the moment she'd dreaded had arrived.

"What happened to Mr. Elwood?" Katie whispered anxiously to Chad. She almost felt like scolding him for not having stayed where he was put.

"Got a good start on him," Chad replied cheerfully, patting his zippered portfolio. "You picked another winner for me, Katie. But then the nurse came in and said he had to have his medication and a nap. He has some kind of trouble with his heart. Maybe I can get back to him later today."

"Oh well," Katie said in an even lower voice, "that's okay. Because Mabel Delacorte is down here. She'll be happy to spend some time with you. I *know* she won't mind missing the horse racing."

Kim, meanwhile, was following Katie and Chad's conversation with the eagerness of somebody watching a champion Ping-Pong match. Her eyes went scooting back and forth as she tried to figure out what Katie and Chad were talking about and — even more important — what they were to each other.

As Chad raised his head to look around the room, probably wondering where Mrs. Delacorte was sitting, Kim thrust herself almost directly beneath his chin.

"Hi," she said, looking up brightly. "I'm Kim." She smiled showing small, even, mother-of-pearl teeth, innocent of ugly metal braces. She widened her clear blue-violet eyes and took a couple of curtain calls with her heavily fringed eyelids. "Are you a volunteer here, too?"

Chad gave her a half-smile and cleared his throat. "Er . . . not really. I'm just a sort of general nuisance, I guess."

Katie hoped Chad meant that as a kind of apology to *her* (which really wasn't necessary). She just didn't want him getting conversational with Kim.

"Oh no, you're not," Katie exclaimed emphatically. She turned to Kim. "Chad's doing a special project of his own," she explained briefly. "He's not a regular here at all."

With that, Katie grabbed Chad's arm to lead him away in the direction of Mabel Delacorte. Her plan was to wheel Mrs. Delacorte into the sun room for Chad's interview and, hopefully, for the picture-taking she planned. Jacqui would need a couple of people in the main lounge to collect the money from the patients for their horse-racing bets and to move the horses forward as the numbers were called. But she could certainly manage with Tracy and Kim. She wouldn't need Katie as well.

The sun room was brighter today than it had been during the grimness of the long Hooperville winter. With Chad at her side, Katie wheeled Mabel Delacorte into the lightest corner and positioned her carefully. There was no one else in the room.

"Before you start, Chad," Katie said almost shyly, reaching for her shoulder bag, "I promised Mrs. Delacorte I'd take her photo today."

Mrs. Delacorte held up her hand. "But I also made a special request, Chad. I want *you* to take a picture with me. Now wait, both of you. Let me just see what repairs are needed." She whipped out her purse mirror. "My lipstick's not smeared, is it,

Katie, dear? These silly eyes of mine make such a blur of everything, I can't tell the difference."

Obligingly, Katie checked Mrs. Delacorte's makeup. Then she backed away and got into a crouch, level with the height of the wheelchair. Out of the corner of her eye, she saw Chad nod approvingly and put up two fingers. She realized his signal meant that he wanted her to take *two* photos, one of them for his oral history file.

Click. Katie couldn't help thinking of that awful morning in the Take-Your-Own-Photo booth when she had been spied on by that twerp, Rob Garrett. She was so much closer to her goal now. Closer and yet . . . far away. How was she going to get that picture of just Chad and herself?

Although she was nervous, Katie managed to snap three pictures of Mabel Delacorte and all of them were good. She, Chad, and Mrs. Delacorte would each be able to keep one.

"Now," Mrs. Delacorte said, waggling her fingers for Chad to come closer, "I want that photo with my best beau." Her eyes danced. For a moment she looked like a wicked forty instead of a withered ninety-two. All this comes, Katie told herself, from holding on to that dream of hers. Whatever it is.

When Katie saw Chad's face in the viewfinder alongside Mabel Delacorte's, she shuddered with a tiny thrill of delight. She felt as though she was about to capture Chad Hollister's very soul. Wasn't that what people in certain parts of the world believed happened to you when somebody took your picture? Once your image was "stolen," you were . . . possessed.

With a sudden, fierce urgency, Katie clicked the

shutter. A few moments later, with Chad looking over her shoulder, she held up the finished photo for Mabel Delacorte to see.

"Give it a minute or two to dry," Katie warned, as Mrs. Delacorte reached for it with clawlike fingers tipped in Regency Pink nail polish. "Now let me take one or two more," Katie begged, getting back into shooting position and motioning Chad to stand next to Mrs. Delacorte as before. She *had* to have one for herself and she'd have to take one to offer Chad, of course. She hoped he wasn't getting impatient. She still had to somehow get the picture she really wanted, of just the two of them. . . .

"Oh, so *this* is where you are!"

Katie turned abruptly, without having snapped the picture. Tracy Palowski stood at the entrance to the sun room, her hands on her hips, her expression pouty.

"Miss Beamish had me looking all over the place for you." Tracy was pointing at Katie but her gaze was already on Chad. Unlike Kim, she hadn't gotten a really close-up look at him in the main lounge. Now she was eyeing him avidly.

Camera in hand, Katie took a few steps toward Tracy. "What does she want?"

Tracy, still focused on Chad, shot Katie an annoyed look. "What do you think she wants? She needs you to help with that game out there. Kim and I never even saw it played before. Do you know I went knocking on the doors in the ladies' room to try to find you? By the way, you could introduce me."

Katie was beginning to seethe at Tracy. She knew

102

very well Tracy wasn't asking to be introduced to Mabel Delacorte. Katie glanced over her shoulder to where Chad had remained near Mrs. Delacorte's chair. "Tracy, this is . . . Chad."

"Nice name," Tracy said, accenting the "nice." Chad nodded politely. "Were you guys taking pictures in here or what?" Tracy wanted to know.

On a sudden impulse, Katie marched over to where Tracy stood. She lifted the camera strap from around her neck. "Yes," she said. "They're for a special project Chad is doing. And we need one more. You could take it for us."

"Oh?" Tracy said with surprise as she took the camera from Katie. "Well, I might be able to do that. What did you want me to take?"

"Us," Katie said boldly. Had the moment really come at last? She led Tracy to the spot where she had been taking photographs, showed her how to press the shutter release, and ran back to stand alongside Chad, on the far side of Mrs. Delacorte's wheelchair. Katie figured that as long as she and Chad were next to each other, she might be able to cut Mrs. Delacorte out of the picture for the Romantic Couples Contest.

Tracy suddenly seemed uncertain. "I . . . I can't get all three of you in the picture," she said, peering into the viewfinder. She looked up. "Listen, I'm really not too good at this. Why doesn't Chad take the picture?"

"Because," Katie replied through clenched teeth, "Chad needs to be in it."

"Then why don't you take it, Katie?" Tracy asked with an innocent air.

"Because," Katie said, feeling her temper begin

103

to flare, "*I* have to be in it, too." Chad turned to look at Katie questioningly, but she just didn't care. She only wished she could have instructed Tracy to leave Mabel Delacorte out of this one. But of course she couldn't do that.

"Oh well," Tracy said, shifting the camera around some more as she searched the viewfinder for the picture she was supposed to take. "It's your funeral. Here goes."

Katie watched Tracy thump the shutter button hard enough to shake the camera. She might have blurred the photo. And who knew what she'd gotten in the frame? Was Tracy really that dumb about using a camera, or was she putting it on just to ruin things for Katie?

In a few moments the picture would be developed and Katie would know. But she had a hunch that Tracy, who'd already left the room with an impatient look at Katie and a warm backward glance at Chad, had foretold the result with those three ominous words of hers: "It's your funeral."

CHAPTER
14

"Irma, I've got to talk to you."

It was Sunday morning and Katie couldn't restrain herself from making an early phone call to Irma. All of the events of yesterday had been bubbling around in her head the entire night. Her brain felt like a seething cauldron.

For one thing, Katie had been steadily filling up with guilt at having locked Irma out of so many corners of her life. She had already resolved that she was going to explain to Irma about her Saturday-afternoon volunteering at the Sunnyside. And now she wanted to make sure that Irma heard it from her rather than from Tracy and Kim at school on Monday.

Katie's biggest uncovered secret since yesterday, of course, was Chad. She *should* have told Irma about him earlier. But Katie found it just as hard to talk about bad experiences with boys, like her fight with Rob, as about good ones. She still had trouble convincing herself that Chad was real. Suppose she told about him and the very next minute he simply vanished like a dream?

As Katie had feared, Irma still sounded hurt about Katie's not having gone to the mall with her. "Yesterday you told *me* not to call you so early. What do you want?"

Katie guessed she deserved Irma's coolness, even though she'd been secretive with Irma *not* to hurt Irma but to protect herself. She could only think of the lines from Sir Walter Scott that she'd learned in seventh grade:

> *Oh, what a tangled web we weave*
> *When first we practice to deceive!*

"Irma," Katie began hesitantly, "it's sort of too much to go through on the telephone. If you wanted to go the mall today . . ."

"Uh-uh," Irma replied quickly. "I told you yesterday that I couldn't."

"Oh," Katie said, trying to sound chatty, "did you go and get that stuff exchanged yesterday? That's partly what I wanted to talk to you about."

"I went," Irma said. Katie had the feeling that Irma was about to say something else but stopped herself.

"If you come over now," Irma went on, after a pause, "we could talk here for a while. But not this afternoon. I'm going somewhere with my family."

Fair enough, Katie thought. She had an awful lot

to tell Irma, besides letting her know how much she appreciated her as a long-suffering friend. Irma *had* put up with a lot from Katie. Funny that she'd only just gotten mad now about the mall episode. Maybe her "new look" was stiffening her pride. She was a new "no-nerd" Irma.

Half an hour later, Katie rang the doorbell of the old house that the DeWitts had bought when they moved to town. It had long been known in Hooperville as the "gingerbread house" because of the carved wooden cornices and fancy bell-shaped cupolas that decorated it. For all its frills, the house was high and narrow, almost squeezed together, like a church. Katie had seen it from the outside but never visited.

Irma's father opened the door. He was tall, pale, and balding, with eyeglasses and a dark beard. Katie thought he looked like a college professor but remembered that Irma had told her he was an engineer.

Mr. DeWitt smiled in answer to her slightly breathless, "I'm Katie," and waved her inside. From the end of a long hallway, Irma's mother called out a cheery greeting. At least Irma's parents didn't seem to be mad at her.

A moment later Irma appeared from the direction of what must have been the kitchen. Contrasted with the outside, the inside of Irma's house was surprisingly bare and simple. Most of the wooden furniture was country-made and hand-rubbed. And the fabrics and hangings, mainly in earth colors, looked like they'd been woven on Irma's mother's loom. Irma herself, though, was in a new pair of jeans and a pale pink top that Katie hadn't seen before. Her hair was definitely growing longer. With her dark bangs she almost had a Cleopatra look. Katie really liked the honest, hand-crafted look of the furnishings in Irma's house. But she could understand Irma's not wanting to wear things like that. They had made Irma stand out in school like a sore thumb. And, even worse, they had probably made her *think* less of herself.

"We can talk in here," Irma said, leading Katie into the living room. Katie realized she wasn't going to be invited upstairs to the intimacy of Irma's room. Irma's parents had disappeared, back to whatever they were busy with before she arrived.

Katie sat down gingerly at one end of a firm-cushioned sofa covered in rust-colored tweed. Irma curled up in an armchair.

"That's a great-looking sweater you're wearing," Katie remarked. "New?"

Irma nodded. "I picked it out myself yesterday." She tossed her head. "I guess I haven't got the world's worst taste."

"Nobody said you had," Katie remarked hastily. "I'm really sorry I couldn't spend the day with you at the mall. That's one of the things I came over to . . . to tell you about."

Irma shifted her body indifferently. "Oh, that's okay," she said with a trace of bitterness that Katie had never seen in her before. "I guess you have a right to your own life."

Katie gulped. "You're mad at me, Irma, aren't you? It's the first time you ever acted like this. Not that . . . I don't deserve it. I know I kept a lot of secrets from you."

Irma's expression remained stony.

"Please," Katie said, leaning forward anxiously, "let me explain about yesterday. Well . . . about all those Saturdays when I told you I was busy. See, I'm a . . . a junior volunteer over at this nursing home here in Hooperville. You know, a place where old people, sick people live. . . ."

Katie paused waiting for some reaction from Irma. But all Irma said was, "So?"

"Okay, okay." Katie leaned back, in frustration. "I know it's no big deal. I *could* have told you about it. I could have even asked you if you wanted to go along with me. But . . . I didn't. I sort of wanted my own 'space.' "

Irma's dark eyes remained fixed on Katie. Her look was sphinxlike. Would Katie ever get her to forgive her?

"That's . . . just the way I am, Irma. I *was* going to tell you about it, though. You don't have to believe me, but it's true. Then, yesterday, when I went there, I wished that I had asked you to come along." Katie paused, thinking wistfully of how nice that would have been. "Some kids turned up there who you know," she added.

Irma tilted her head slightly. "Who?" she asked coolly.

Katie pressed her lips together in exasperation. "Two girls from school. Tracy Palowski and Kim Brewer. Can you imagine, Irma? I was just furious."

Irma, although still distant, looked puzzled. "But why, Katie? It's a free country. I guess if they wanted to be volunteers, nobody could really stop them." She narrowed her eyes slightly. "Only how did they find out about the place?"

Katie shook her head vigorously. "Not through

me, Irma. Please believe that. You've *got* to believe that. When I got there I found the two of them giggling in the entrance, acting really dumb. They'd been sent over by some aunt of Tracy's who works there. They didn't even *want* to come."

Irma sighed. "Well, I still don't see why you should have been so upset." She folded her arms across her chest and looked away, as if to say, "It's no business of mine." Katie could sense Irma's pain and hurt, her feeling of having been left out of Katie's life, which she had never expressed until now.

"I'm 'upset,' Irma, because they're not my friends and you are. And I should have asked you if you wanted to be a volunteer there, and I didn't. And . . . and . . . I'm asking you now."

Irma flashed a sorrowful look at Katie.

"Oh please, Irma," Katie pleaded. "Don't say it's too late. I've been so . . . crazy lately. I couldn't concentrate on anything. I didn't mean to ignore you. It was just . . . circumstances." Katie's voice dropped. "I want you for a friend."

"Oh?" Irma said quietly. Her tone didn't seem as challenging and bitter as it had a moment earlier. Maybe she was a little more ready to hear Katie out.

"Listen," Katie said with new hope, "there's a special reason I want you to come to the nursing home with me next Saturday. There's somebody there I want you to meet." Her voice trailed off a bit. "If only he's there next time. . . ."

Irma showed a faint spark of interest. "There are boy volunteers, too?"

Katie shook her head. "No. At least I never met any. This boy is doing a . . . a high-school research project there. He's interviewing patients for their life stories. His name is . . . Chad Hollister."

With trembling hands, Katie began to dig distractedly in her purse. She drew the picture taken by Tracy Palowski out of an envelope and handed it to Irma. "Please," she said, "try not to get fingerprints on it. It's the only picture of him I may ever . . . have."

Irma gave Katie a look of mild alarm, as she noticed the shakiness in her hands and also in her voice. Katie herself couldn't bear to look at the picture. She sat back, trying to relax, waiting for Irma's reaction.

"So-o-o," Irma said very slowly, "this is the second big secret you've been keeping from me, Katie." But, looking at the picture, she appeared fairly calm. In fact, her lips parted in a faint smile and her eyes began to light up.

"Well," Katie said, leaning forward. "What do you think? I only met him last week and he still doesn't seem . . . real to me. So don't be mad about my not saying anything until now."

Irma's eyes lingered on the photograph. Chad's magic seemed to be working on her, too. "He's . . . gorgeous," she declared with emphasis. "*Gorgeous.* But who are the other people in the picture?"

Katie found herself pouring out the whole story to Irma. "Tracy Palowski took that picture. I swear, Irma, she messed it up on purpose. She *said* she couldn't get all three of us in. That's a tiny little piece of *me* on Chad's right side. And that's Mabel Delacorte, one of the patients, in the wheelchair on his left. You can see there was *plenty* of room for Tracy to fit all of me in. But she didn't."

Irma handed the photo back to Katie. She appeared truly concerned about Katie's unhappiness. Katie gave her a grateful look as she tucked the picture away. Were they really friends now, she wondered, friends on an equal footing? Irma had once needed Katie more than Katie needed Irma. Now the tables were turned.

"I don't understand," Irma said. "Why was it so important, Katie, for you to be in the picture? If all you wanted was a good picture of him, you've got it. You could cut away the part of you that's in it and also the lady in the wheelchair."

Katie looked up plaintively. "Irma, I *have* to be in the picture with Chad. That's the whole point, on account of the . . . the . . ."

Irma, who was just about to relax with a stretch, dropped her arms suddenly. "The what?" she asked suspiciously. "Something else you didn't tell me about, Katie?"

"Yes," Katie blurted helplessly. "I might as well tell you. The Romantic Couples Contest."

Irma slouched into her chair with an expression of strained-to-the-breaking-point endurance on her face. Was she going to get mad at Katie all over again? "Honestly, Katie Dinkerhoff," she said, "you are the most secretive person I ever met. That makes *three* things you never told me that I just found out about today — what you've been doing on Saturdays, the boy you met, and this . . . this contest you're in."

"I know, I know," Katie said. "I've been awful, Irma. But I'm that way with everybody, not just you. My Aunt Zoe's the only one who knows about Chad and the . . . the contest. And she found out

112

by pure accident. I don't like to tell people the . . . the things I do because I'm afraid they won't come out right."

Irma crossed her arms and regarded Katie silently. She didn't seem *too* angry, but her look said something like, "Well, what are you going to do about it now?"

"I'm going to tell you everything," Katie declared, breaking the silence between them. "*Everything*, Irma. Right from the start. . . ."

Twenty minutes later, Irma saw Katie to the door.

"I'll phone Jacqui Beamish tomorrow," Katie promised, "and tell her I'm bringing a new teen volunteer next Saturday. She'll be really happy. I know she thought Tracy and Kim were a couple of airheads. Which they are."

Irma nodded, not bothering to hide a pleased smile. "Well, it ought to be . . . interesting," she said. "Especially if Chad is there."

"Oh, I'm pretty sure he will be," Katie sighed. "He did some more tape-recording with Mrs. Delacorte yesterday. But he never got back to interviewing Mr. Elwood. And he might even want to do more people. The information he gets is going into the county records. It *might* become part of a time capsule or something." Katie knew her cheeks were flushed and her eyes were dancing. How else could it be when she was talking about Chad?

Irma looked at Katie with an indulgent expression. "But what are you going to do about getting a picture of the two of you for the Romantic Couples Contest?" she asked.

Katie shrugged. "I don't know. I have to think

about that some more. It's . . . embarrassing. I can't keep on asking Chad to pose for pictures with me."

"Maybe," Irma said thoughtfully, "I could help you."

Katie looked at her. "How?"

"Oh, I'll try to work something out. I'm pretty good at photography. Why don't you bring your camera along . . . and we'll see."

Even though Irma's words were vague, Katie sensed an air of confidence about her. But no matter how things turned out, Katie was touched by Irma's offer. Impulsively, she hugged her. "You're a real friend, Irma," she whispered.

But Irma only laughed, as she hugged Katie back. "You're not so bad, either. Even though you seem to *love* keeping secrets, I figure you're still okay."

Tears prickled at Katie's eyelids as she remembered how she'd once called Irma a nerd. She was glad that she was already halfway down the steps of the "gingerbread house" and that Irma couldn't see her face.

CHAPTER
15

It was Monday lunchtime in the school cafeteria. Irma, who was on the food line directly in front of Katie, slid her tray along the ledge of the steam table and reached for a plate of frankfurters and sauerkraut. Katie nudged her lightly and gave her a surprised look. Irma usually chose health-type lunches like cottage cheese salads and bran muffins. But ever since she'd changed her style of dress, Katie noticed Irma seemed to be changing her diet as well.

Irma merely smiled mischievously. "I know you won't tell my mother, Katie. You're such a good secret-keeper."

Irma had been making little remarks like that ever since yesterday when Katie had told her all about the Sunnyside and Chad and the Romantic Couples Contest. Katie knew she had it coming for not having confided in Irma a long time ago. She sighed and put the skimpiest plate of salad she could find on her tray. Her appetite, never very big, was definitely in a slump these days. Especially when she thought about Chad, which was all the time.

"Now let's be very careful where we sit," Katie cautioned Irma, as they came off the cashier's line. "We want to be as far away as possible from Tracy and Kim's table. I just don't want to see those two. A hundred years from now would be too soon." Fortunately, Tracy and Kim hadn't been in any of Katie's Monday morning classes.

Irma pointed with her chin toward an empty corner table and Katie followed her to it. "Let's sit with our backs to the rest of the lunchroom," Katie suggested.

Irma giggled. "That might guarantee *your* not seeing *them*. But it won't work vice versa." She indulged Katie anyhow and they sat side by side facing a cinder-block wall painted mustard yellow.

"Things certainly have changed," Irma remarked, biting into a frankfurter and squirting hot, salty juice in Katie's direction. "I remember when you were always creeping around after those two, making us sit at the same table so it would look like we were a part of their crowd."

"Oh honestly, Irma," Katie groaned, "please stop rubbing it in. You can't imagine how uncomfortable they make me. You should have seen Kim batting her eyelashes at Chad on Saturday."

Irma nodded sympathetically and went on eating. Katie began chewing on a celery stick. Between her second and third crunch, she heard a shrieky laugh behind her and clutched Irma's sleeve. "*Don't* turn around. It might be them."

But Irma had already turned. It was too late, anyway. Tracy and Kim stood directly behind them, their lunch trays in their hands.

"Ooh," Kim cried out, "here you are. Can we sit with you?"

Before Katie or Irma could say anything, the two girls slid onto the bench across the table from them.

"How come you picked such an out-of-the-way table?" Kim wanted to know. "Tracy and I saw you on line ahead of us. But then we lost you." She turned to Irma. "You're Katie's friend Irma, aren't you? Hi."

Irma nodded while Tracy and Kim eyed her appraisingly. "You're letting your hair grow," Tracy commented. "Looks good with those bangs. Reminds me of somebody on TV. I can't think who."

Katie was silent. She hadn't told Irma that Kim Brewer had called her a Raggedy Ann doll when she had her old haircut.

Tracy began pushing the food around on her plate. "So," she said, tossing Katie a private look, "how did the . . . um, picture I took on Saturday come out?"

Katie placed a hand on Irma's shoulder. "You can talk in front of Irma. She knows all about it."

Kim shot Katie an excited glance. "Does she know about *him*?"

Irma shook her head yes, pleased to be in on Katie's secret.

"But," Kim demanded, "has she *met* him?"

"Not yet," Katie replied. "But soon."

Tracy was chewing her food slowly. "You still didn't tell me about the picture," she reminded Katie. "Have you got it with you?"

Katie shook her head. "Uh-uh. But *you* should know what it looks like. You took it, after all."

Kim searched Katie's face. "You sound mad. What did Tracy do wrong?"

"She knows," Katie murmured accusingly. "She left me out of it almost completely."

Tracy tossed her head. "Oh, that's ridiculous. I certainly didn't do it on purpose. It's hard to get three people in one picture."

"That," Katie said pointedly, "is the stupidest thing I ever heard."

"Sshh, sshh," Kim hissed, patting the air for peace. "What a dumb thing to fight about. If you bring your camera next week, Katie, I'll take a picture of you and Chad."

"Thanks," Katie replied. "But that won't be necessary. Irma can do it. She'll be there next Saturday."

"Ohh," Kim said with mild surprise. "So Irma's going to be a volunteer, too. That'll make four of us. You don't think that might be too many?"

"No," Katie retorted. "Not at all. I already phoned Jacqui Beamish this morning about Irma's coming. She said 'fine.' That way I can take more time helping Chad with his work." Katie knew she shouldn't be flaunting her special relationship with Chad in front of Tracy and Kim. It was asking for trouble. But she just couldn't help it. Tracy's eyes were cool and sharklike. And Kim's were kittenish and glittering. Katie wanted to remind them that *she* had seen Chad first. As far as she was concerned, he was hers.

Tracy flung her hair back again and regarded Katie with more friendliness. "So who else do you know from Hooperville High? Have you met any of Chad's friends yet?"

Katie exchanged glances with Irma, who, from the expression in her eyes, had also caught the meaning in Tracy's question. If Kim and Tracy weren't going to be able to get Chad for themselves, they hoped to use Katie as bait for meeting other high-school boys. They were probably just as bored with ninth-grade boys as all the other ninth-grade girls.

"So far," Katie said, choosing her words carefully, "we've talked mostly about Chad's research project. He's very serious about his work."

Kim threw Tracy a knowing glance. "You haven't really . . . dated yet, have you?" Kim inquired.

Irma started to titter in a purposely silly way. "My goodness," she said, "it sounds like you two are giving Katie the third degree. She doesn't have to answer questions like that about her private life. Do you, Katie?"

Kim giggled lightly. "Oops, sorry. I just thought we were all friends here. Maybe I was wrong."

At that moment Tracy, who like Kim was facing into the lunchroom, half-rose from her seat waving her right arm frantically. "Hey!" she shouted. "We're over here. This way."

Katie turned, relieved and grateful that Irma had gotten her off the hook. She wondered who Tracy was waving to. But the cafeteria had become very crowded and Katie couldn't spot anyone in particular. Wasn't it amazing how Tracy and Kim had sniffed her out, though, once they'd found out about Chad? She knew very well that they would have gone right on ignoring her and Irma if not for him.

By this time, Kim too was waving. "Sit here," she shouted, patting the seat beside her. "We have space."

Irma, who had also turned around to look, gave Katie a poke. "It's Rob Garrett and some other kids," she said with a look of mild alarm. "Do you want to leave?"

Katie could feel the back of her neck stiffen. Rob Garrett had kept a low profile all last week. And even if Katie had come face to face with him, she felt she could have withered him with a single sneer. But now, with Kim and Tracy and his other friends around, she'd be outnumbered. Still, she was determined to hold her ground.

"No," she hissed back at Irma. "We were here first."

Irma, her head still turned to look behind her, continued to report in a whisper. "The other boys with him aren't coming. Just Rob."

Katie was only slightly less tense. She wondered if one of the boys with Rob had been his partner in the spying incident at the Take-Your-Own-Photo booth in the mall.

Suddenly Rob was standing just behind Kim and Tracy, a can of soda in his hand. He seemed shocked to find himself staring directly at Katie.

Katie kept a straight face, her eyes somber. "Oh, hi," Rob said uncomfortably, trying for a casual effect. His cheeks didn't have that pinkish flush that Katie had found rather babyish in spite of his good looks. In fact, Rob was rather pale today.

"Sit down, Rob," Kim squeaked affably, making a cozy space between Tracy and herself. Rob lifted one long leg after the other over the bench and dropped down onto it, clunking his can of soda onto the table in front of him.

"This is Katie and this is Irma," Kim said, pointing to each of them in turn. "Maybe you've seen them around." She threw an arm loosely around Rob's neck. "Rob Garrett, the cutest guy in the whole ninth grade. And the best athlete. Tracy and I are both crazy about him." She glanced past Rob at Tracy. "Aren't we, Tray? We're like a threesome that's going steady. Rob can't decide which of us he likes better. So we're *both* his girlfriend."

Rob began to find his tongue. "Yeah," he complained, circling each of them around the waist. "Trouble is you're too much alike. That's why I can't decide. I like you both. I guess what I really need is somebody different."

"Ooh," Kim said, tugging playfully at Rob's ear, "don't look at Katie. Irma maybe, but not Katie. Because she's taken. Did you know she's got a boyfriend who's a high-school sophomore?"

Rob threw Katie a quick glance. Did he remember the day he'd told her she looked like a seventh grader, Katie wondered?

"And that's not even half of it," Tracy added, keeping her eyes on Katie's face. "Katie's boyfriend is so-o-o handsome. And *very* serious and grown up." Tracy peered around in front of Rob, cupped her hand alongside her mouth, and said in a voice loud enough for Katie and Irma to hear, "Kim and I are planning to steal him from her one of these days, if we can. Isn't that right, Kimmie?"

"Oh honestly," Irma said, suddenly rising from the table and almost stumbling backward. "I don't think any of this talk is the least bit funny. Maybe we should go, Katie. I'm done eating. Are you?"

Even Katie was surprised at Irma's outburst. All at once both Kim and Tracy were on their feet, too, waving their arms at Irma. "Oh, calm down," Kim said bossily to Irma. "Katie knows we're only teasing, don't you, Katie?"

"Of course," Tracy added, before Katie could get a word in, "if Katie would introduce us to some of Chad's high-school friends, we might not even be *thinking* of trying to steal Chad. They'd have to be a lot like him, though," she warned.

Blackmail, Katie thought with horror. That was exactly what it was. Tracy and Kim weren't going to let go when it came to Chad. True, she had Irma to keep a crafty eye out and to stand up for her. But would that be enough?

Rob Garrett, meantime, no longer held captive by Tracy and Kim, began to pull his legs out from under the table. He leaped backward over the bench and said almost confidentially to Katie, who was the only person still sitting, "I don't know what this is all about. But I'm getting out of here fast."

"You ought to," Katie retorted. "I don't know where you even get the nerve to talk to me."

Rob threw up his hands. "What did I do now? Gee, you really have got the most redheaded temper I ever saw. A person can't say a word to you."

"A word!" Katie exclaimed, getting to her feet. By now, Irma, Kim, and Tracy had left their places and were standing a short distance from the table

122

having a free-for-all of accusations about who had said what to hurt somebody else's feelings.

Katie jammed her knuckles against her waist. If she was going to give Rob Garrett what-for, now was as good a time as any. "Maybe I could just remind you, Rob Garrett, of a very few choice words that *you* used to me a short while back. Or have you forgotten that when I went over to talk to you in study hall, with all good intentions, you called me a 'pipsqueak' *and* a 'seventh grader' *and* 'metal-mouth' *and* 'railroad tracks'? You called my friend Irma a 'klutz.' You tried to trip me up in the study-hall aisle. *And,* last but not least, you and some other juvenile creep spied on me at the mall last week when I was trying to get my picture taken."

Rob went a little white around the mouth at Katie's last statement.

"Oh," she said, narrowing her eyes, "I guess you thought I didn't know about that."

Rob was silent for a few moments. Then he flung his hands in the air as if to ward off a swarm of buzzing insects. "Girls!" he exclaimed disgustedly. "They're all crazy." He glanced over to where Tracy, Kim, and Irma were still arguing. "Crazy," he repeated, his voice breaking slightly. "And *you,*" he said hotly, aiming a finger at Katie, "don't even know how to take a joke. That's all it was ever supposed to be. A joke." He slapped one hand against his forehead in a gesture of frustration. "Aw, lemme outa here!"

"Some joke," Katie called after him as he loped away. "What would *you* ever know about a person's feelings!"

Exhausted, Katie flopped down again on the bench.

Neither Tracy nor Kim, nor even Irma, had noticed Rob's departure. At least, Katie thought, she had settled her score with him. She even had the tiniest suspicion that Rob Garrett had been a little bit interested in her and that he had shown it in the only way he knew, by teasing and trying to put her down. For all his good looks, Rob had behaved like a big baby. It was time for him to grow up.

By instant contrast, Katie of course thought of Chad and of the problem at hand. How, she wondered, even with Irma's help, was she ever going to get Kim and Tracy off her back so she could concentrate on really trying to learn his feelings about her?

CHAPTER
16

Irma flipped the postcard from the Romantic Couples Contest from front to back, and stared once again at the printed message on the reverse side.

"And this is all you've heard from them so far, Katie?"

It was later in the week and Katie and Irma were in Katie's room, the "sardine can," presumably to rehearse a Spanish-conversation playlet that Señora McCardle had assigned. It had been agreed in class that they would act out a scene in a dress shop, with Irma as the customer and Katie as the sales-clerk. All in Spanish, of course.

"The entry blank should come any day now, Irma, don't you see?" Katie replied. "I want to be ready so I can mail it off right away. That's why I thought maybe we could also get a little work in today on the fifty-word essay on how we met — um, Chad and I — and what it feels like to be part of a couple. I'm supposed to send that in along with the picture."

Irma was examining the front of the card now. " 'K.T. Dinkerhoff.' That's cute," she mused.

Katie was beginning to get impatient. The afternoon was going and so far they hadn't done much of anything. Irma seemed in a lazy mood. "Well," Katie urged, "what do you think?"

Irma looked up. "About what?"

"What I just said," Katie pressed her. "The fifty words about how it feels to be part of a couple."

Irma shrugged. "I don't know, Katie. How *does* it feel?"

"Irma," Katie replied with exasperation, "how should *I* know? I don't even know if Chad and I are a couple . . . yet. I'm trying to . . . to make it happen. But I can't just wait around. Meantime I have to write those fifty words, and I guess I'll just have to use my imagination."

Katie had become slightly worried as the week wore on for, unlike last week, Chad hadn't phoned her at all. Of course, he *had* said last Saturday, after the picture-taking with Mrs. Delacorte (which had so disappointed Katie), that he would be back the following week to see Mr. Elwood. But Katie could have used some reassuring. Chad was still a closed book to her. He was businesslike most of the time, yet gave her deeply appraising looks at other times. What was really going on in his head?

"Hmmm," Irma remarked, "you'll have to, won't you? I mean, use your imagination. I'm sort of wondering, Katie, how you ever got this idea of entering the contest in the first place."

Katie folded her arms across her chest. "I *told* you, Irma. I found an announcement about it in Mabel Delacorte's paperback book and I mailed it in."

"I know," Irma said. "But I see lots of contests being advertised all over the place. 'Write a jingle about Purple-Sparkle Dishwashing Liquid and win a mink coat.' That kind of thing. I'd never dream of entering."

"Ah!" Katie exclaimed, pointing a finger at Irma. "That's the key word you just used. *Dream.* You have to have a dream, Irma."

"Well," Irma drawled, "which dream got you started? The one about going to New York City for a glamorous weekend or the one about being part of a romantic couple?"

Katie leaned back against Aunt Zoe's cross-stitch cushions. "First," she said thoughtfully, "I guess it was the idea of the trip itself because I didn't even know of a possible boyfriend at the time. I've hardly ever been out of Hooperville. Wouldn't you just love going to a big city, not as some little nobody, but as a sort of special guest? Almost like a celebrity?"

Irma nodded. "Sounds good."

"But then," Katie went on, "I realized I wouldn't stand a chance of even entering the contest if I didn't find some boy. So I started to work on that."

Irma gave Katie a quizzical look. "How?"

Katie suddenly realized that she was very close to giving away her very last secret to Irma. Just about eighteen inches from her left elbow was the sweater drawer with her diary in it. Katie took a deep breath and slowly pulled open the drawer. Irma's loyalty, after the way that Katie had treated her, was no small thing. She deserved Katie's last confidence — provided Katie was careful to show her only the pages that wouldn't hurt her feelings.

There was the entry for Tuesday, March 12, for example:

> *Today I got rid of Irma and I actually went over and* talked *to Rob Garrett.* . . .

She wouldn't show Irma that one. Even though Irma had probably suspected it, it would prove that Katie had purposely sent Irma up to the fifth floor with her library books that day.

The entry for Saturday, March 16, though, wasn't too dangerous to show Irma. It mentioned Katie's disgust with ninth-grade boys and her plan for going to the mall to try to meet somebody new and to visit the Take-Your-Own-Photo alcove. It ended with the prophetic:

> *Today I met somebody new. And very nice!*

Katie took the plunge. She drew her diary out of the drawer and, before Irma realized what was happening, opened to the part she wanted her to see.

"Read this," Katie said. "It's my secret diary. Nobody in the world has ever seen it before. It'll answer your question about 'how,' Irma." She pointed to the entry that started with:

Irma gave Katie a brief, startled glance. Then she leaned over and began to devour what Katie had written on the page. When she had finished, she looked up openmouthed. "Wow, that was the day I went to the mall with my mother. Were you in the photo place, Katie, when Rob. . . ?"

Katie nodded slowly.

"So it was *you* that he and this other kid were peeking in at just before they ran past. . . ."

"Um-hmmm," Katie said. "And when I met you and you mentioned what you had just seen, I realized it *had* been Rob. Up to that moment I didn't know who it was, and then I got *so* mad. But, Irma, you're missing the whole point. None of that stuff with Rob is important anymore. I really told him off in the lunchroom the other day when you were hassling with Tracy and Kim. What you don't realize, Irma, is that I wrote this whole thing" — Katie ran her hand down the page — "the day *before* it happened. Not on Saturday the sixteenth, but on *Friday the fifteenth*."

Irma gave Katie a disbelieving look. "You mean you wrote that you were going to meet Chad the day *before* you actually met him. How could you do that? It sounds . . . witchy."

"I . . . was desperate, Irma," Katie explained. "I wasn't trying to pull some crystal-ball trick, like foretelling the future. At the same time, I thought that if I *said* I was going to meet somebody wonderful, I'd sort of *force* it to happen."

"That's crazy," Irma retorted. "If nobody great came along that day, there simply wouldn't have been anybody to meet. I think you were just lucky, Katie. If you *could* make things happen by writing them down ahead of time, how come you didn't get a terrific photo of you and Chad last Saturday for the contest?"

Katie scrambled for the next page of her diary. Irma's question was a good one. "I know I wrote about that, Irma."

She and Irma bent their heads over the following page on which Katie had written the Friday evening before the picture-taking. " 'Today, Saturday,' " Katie read out loud, " 'I saw him again at the Sunnyside Nursing Home where we met.' " That part had certainly come true.

" '*And,*' " Irma continued, reading from the same paragraph, " 'we had a picture taken — together!' "

Irma stared at Katie and Katie stared back. "Now why didn't *that* come true?" Katie pondered. "It should have happened just the way I wrote it."

Irma, who seemed to have entered into the spirit of Katie's secret diary, considered this for a moment. "I know why," Irma said, her eyes lighting up. "You wrote it wrong, Katie. You and Chad *posed* for a picture of the two of you. You were standing side by side but it didn't come out that way. Most of you was missing. You should have written, 'A picture was taken that has Chad and me in it, just right for the Romantic Couples Contest.' Or some such thing."

Katie punched the surface of the studio bed on which they were sitting. "You're right. You're pretty smart, Irma. I think I'll let *you* start writing in my diary the day before something important has to happen." She paused and leaned toward Irma. "Now, do you think you can help me with the fifty words? I bet I'd win if you did."

Before Irma had a chance to answer, footsteps came clattering along the upstairs hallway and Babette peered in at the doorway of Katie's room.

"Aha. I thought I heard familiar voices in here. Lloyd Huntziger just canceled his mambo lesson. So I thought I'd come up and wash my hair instead. How nice to see you, Irma."

Babette sounded surprisingly cheerful. Usually she was in a really down mood when one of her elderly students didn't show up for an expensive private session. At the same time, Katie couldn't help tensing up at Irma and her mother's meeting again, even though Babette had been as good as her word so far about not pressuring Katie or her friends anymore. Katie would have to tell her mother that she *had* invited Irma to be a volunteer at the Sunnyside. But not right now.

Irma was grinning almost adoringly at Babette and saying, "Your hair always looks just perfect to me, Mrs. Dinkerhoff."

Babette put her hand up to her golden "chrysanthemum" cut. "Oh well," she said a trifle coquettishly. "I think it's about ready for a little rinse, if you know what I mean." She winked. "I like that new look you're cultivating, Irma. Suits you very well. You're getting to be a very glamorous 'type.' "

"You two sound like a mutual admiration society," Katie said, feeling a little jealous that her mother was paying so much attention to Irma.

"Hmmm," Babette said. She stepped through the doorway, swooped down on Katie, and planted a noisy kiss on her cheek. "No need to feel left out. I love you, too, baby. We both do, don't we, Irma?"

As soon as she was gone, Katie and Irma looked at each other and began to titter. "My mother is weird," Katie remarked.

"I like your mother a lot," Irma said. "Mine's nice, too. But they're so . . . different."

Katie shook her head. "I just realized what a good mood she's been in lately. I can't understand it. Feels like she's been in a bad mood for years. Always worrying about the studio, you know, because it's running downhill and she's losing her students. A lot of them have already ended up at the Sunnyside. I'll show you on Saturday." Katie scratched her temple. "And now this change . . . she really seems . . . happy."

"Hey," Irma suggested, "I just thought of something. Why don't you ask your mother to help you write the fifty words about what it feels like to be part of a couple? She'd know."

Katie laughed. "Oh, Irma, she's been married so long. It's not at all the same. Anyhow," she added, putting her finger to her lips and lowering her voice, "remember that she doesn't know anything about Chad or the contest. Only Zoe knows."

Irma nodded. "Oh, sorry." She glanced at her watch. "Gosh, Katie, it's getting late. I've got to go soon. We'd better run through the dress shop routine for Spanish class. Now, I'll make it easy for you because I'll ask most of the questions. All you'll have to tell me will be practically one-word answers, like color, size, price, and where the fitting room is."

After they'd finished the run-through and Katie

132

saw Irma out the door, she went back to her room with a tremendous feeling of relief. She was glad she didn't have any more secrets from Irma. It felt really good to have a true friend, one who was so amazingly selfless and supportive. How awful Katie had been, pushing Irma away in the days when she'd been stupid enough to think she wanted to be part of the crowd that Tracy and Kim ran around with.

Tracy and Kim. The thought of the two girls gave Katie a leaden feeling in the pit of her stomach. Ever since Monday's episode in the lunchroom, she and Irma had exchanged only a few frozen smiles with them. What was going to happen on Saturday when they all came together at the Sunnyside?

Yet, in spite of the menace of Tracy and Kim, Katie hoped desperately that Chad would show up. If he did, she was almost sure she'd be able to get a truly romantic photo of the two of them. Babette had said she could borrow the camera again, Katie had bought more film for it, and Irma was going to be the photographer.

In fact, before putting her diary away in the drawer, Katie dragged it out from under the bed where she had temporarily hidden it. "I *have* to make it happen this time," she whispered to herself. Then, mustering all her confidence, she wrote down the following for Saturday, March 30 (which was two days from now):

> *At last, I have a wonderful photo of Chad and me to send in to the Romantic Couples Contest. New York City, here we come!*

CHAPTER
17

Katie sat in the darkened main lounge of the Sunnyside Nursing Home watching an old Hollywood movie that Jacqui Beamish had rented for this week's Saturday afternoon "activity." The film, which was in blurry Technicolor and had a scratchy sound track, was a nineteen-fifties musical. But it might just as well have been a tearjerker. In fact, that would have suited Katie's mood better. For it was now after three o'clock, by the flickering light on Katie's wristwatch, and Chad Hollister hadn't yet put in an appearance. And worse, the week had ended without his having called her.

"Irma," Katie sighed, "would you mind taking another look around? Maybe he's just arrived. I'm so worried."

Irma got to her feet. She'd been sitting beside the

movie projector with Katie. Jacqui had left Katie in charge of the picture-showing just in case the film broke or one of the reels on the creaking machine jammed. The room was only partially filled and, as usual, several of the residents sat with drooping heads.

Katie felt trapped by the assignment Jacqui had given her. In a way it was a compliment because she was the most experienced of the teenage volunteers. But, on the other hand, it kept her "in the dark" about what Tracy and Kim were up to. At her last report from Irma, Katie had learned that the two girls had brought a small group of patients down to the arts and crafts room to work on sewing stuffed animals for Sunnyside's Easter bazaar. This was dangerous because Chad might show up at any moment and fall instantly into their clutches.

Katie and Irma had arrived early at the Sunnyside that Saturday so Katie could have plenty of time to acquaint Irma with the place. Jacqui Beamish had given Irma a short welcoming greeting with the words, "I know I can trust any friend of Katie's to be a really responsible volunteer." What Jacqui thought of Tracy and Kim she just wasn't saying. But she had rapidly taken them under her wing the moment they'd arrived.

Katie looked up anxiously as she saw Irma's figure slip back into the darkened lounge and take the long way around behind the rows of wheelchairs to where Katie sat.

"Well?" Katie whispered. "Anything?"

Irma shook her head. "Nope. It's quiet all over and the only man I saw who wasn't a patient was the janitor."

"Did you check the third floor?" Katie pounced. "Just in case he came in and went directly up to Mr. Elwood's room?"

"I did. I did," Irma assured her. "Mr. Elwood was sitting in the day room and he looked annoyed when I asked him if Chad had been there yet. He said something about 'young whippersnappers that seem nice as cream and then never keep their promises.' He was bent over the table writing something, maybe a 'letter to the editor' about Chad." Irma giggled.

Katie merely sighed once again. She'd filled Irma in about Mr. Elwood and Mabel Delacorte, and had introduced her to them when they'd first arrived. And she'd already put Irma through the routine of searching for Chad twice before.

"And what about Tracy and Kim?" Katie asked. She had just taken a quick look at the movie screen on which a flirtatious blonde actress had appeared who reminded her of Tracy. Or Kim. Or both.

"Oh," Irma said, "I only *peeked* into the crafts room. They were in there with Jacqui Beamish helping the patients who are sewing the stuffed animals. They didn't see me." She placed her hand lightly on Katie's arm. "Chad definitely wasn't there. Why don't you relax, Katie? Either he'll turn up or he won't. If he doesn't, he'll probably phone you next week."

"Or he won't," Katie murmured glumly. "Do you realize I don't even have his phone number? And even if I could get it, what good would that do? I need that picture of him — of us — today. I'm all set up for it."

Irma leaned back in her chair. "You know what

you are, Katie? You're too compulsive. You make up your mind how something's supposed to be and then you have a fit if it doesn't come out that way."

Katie turned to Irma as the images on the screen burst into a brassy song-and-dance number. She raised her voice slightly to be heard above the din. "Well what's wrong with going after something you want? Haven't *you* ever done the same thing, Irma?"

Irma shrugged. "Well, in a way." Katie knew Irma couldn't deny that she'd set out to make Katie her friend right from the start. And she'd succeeded.

"Oh, I nearly forgot," Irma added, probably relieved to be changing the subject. "One of the nurses on the third floor said to tell 'the other volunteer' — I guess that means you — that Mabel Delacorte won't be coming down at all today."

Katie looked alarmed. "Why? Is she sick?"

Irma shook her head. "I don't know. I was just getting into the elevator and the door was closing. I couldn't find the 'hold' button fast enough."

Katie stood up. "Well, that does it. I wondered why she didn't come down for the movie. I'll have to go see how she is."

"Oh, Katie," Irma pleaded. "What if this machine breaks? Jacqui Beamish told *you* to stay here with it."

"Usually it breaks every *other* time we use it," Katie told her. "Mabel Delacorte is special. To me and . . . to Chad. I have to make sure she's okay. If the projector busts, Irma, just turn on the lights and put on the TV set. Maybe the same movie is playing on one of the channels and nobody'll even know the difference."

Once she was able to roam freely, Katie felt a lot

better. She furtively checked the crafts room and found everything there to be just as Irma had reported it. Then she tiptoed away and peered into most of the other rooms on the main floor, including the staff lunchroom where she and Chad had had their first eye-to-eye, across-the-table encounter and she had fallen smack-bang in love with him.

After that, Katie got into the elevator and rode up to the third floor. Again, she couldn't help thinking of Chad — the way he'd looked at her last week once they'd found themselves alone, the warmth, in his voice when he'd asked, "How've you been, Katie?" And, struggling to find the perfect word, secretly loving him more than ever, she'd foolishly answered, "Wonderful."

Passing the third-floor day room, Katie saw Mr. Elwood still angrily scribbling away. He probably *was* writing another letter to a newspaper about the indifference of people who seemed to care about you one week and forgot all about you the next. Katie felt almost the same way herself.

At Mabel Delacorte's door, Katie paused. Mrs. Delacorte was seated in her wheelchair, her back to the entrance. The room was filled with the scents of cologne, dusting powder, and perfumed soap, almost strong enough to drown out the powerful disinfectant smell of the corridors at the Sunnyside. Old-fashioned dolls dressed as Spanish dancers lay against the pillows of Mrs. Delacorte's bed. Her night table was cluttered with bottles, tubes, and jars of creams and cosmetics.

Calling out a casual greeting so as not to startle her, Katie came around to the front of Mrs. Delacorte's chair. Mabel Delacorte's face was heavily made up. But her eyes were closed, and they remained that way.

"Mrs. Delacorte?" Katie inquired in a hushed voice. She was listening for the sound of the "z-z-z-z-z humff . . . z-z-z-z-z humff" that she had heard the last time Mabel Delacorte had dozed off. That had been when Katie was reading *Love's Luscious Longing* to her down in the sun room. Katie remembered that Mrs. Delacorte had been sitting up as straight then as she was now. No droopy-headed snoozing for her. Even in sleep she proudly kept up appearances.

Katie leaned a little bit closer. But there was no "z-z-z-z-z humff" to be heard. There wasn't even, as far as Katie could tell, the sound of normal breathing. Katie felt a stab of panic. She wasn't supposed to check a patient's pulse or anything like that. She started out of the room to call the nurse.

"Where are you going?" came a startlingly deep voice from the padded lining of the wheelchair. Katie jolted to a stop. Mrs. Delacorte peered around the side of the chair and curled a bony finger at Katie. "Come back here, please."

"Oh," Katie breathed with relief. "I was getting worried. I couldn't tell if you were sleeping . . . or what. They told me you weren't coming down at all today."

Mabel Delacorte pointed to the bed opposite her chair. "Sit down a minute, my dear."

Katie perched on the edge of the high, hard hospital bed. At night, the sides were usually put up so the patients wouldn't fall out.

"What . . . is it?" Katie asked, still not sure she shouldn't ring for the nurse. "Did you have a bad turn or something?"

Mabel Delacorte waved her right hand back and forth in denial. "No, no. Nothing physical. I was in a blue funk, that's all. Feeling just terribly depressed. I couldn't shake myself out of it."

"B — But you," Katie began. "You're always so lively. You always say that you're 'holding on to the dream.' "

As soon as Katie said the words, she felt she'd made a terrible mistake. Mabel Delacorte's glance dropped to her lap and her mouth grew bitter.

"Ohh," Katie stammered, "I'm sorry. I only mentioned it because . . . well, I always wondered what dream that was. See, I believe in having a dream, too. In fact, I'm holding on to one myself right now. Very tightly."

Mrs. Delacorte raised her eyes. "Well, you should, at your age. In fact, you'd better. If you don't dream some pretty good dreams now — and work hard to make them come true — you won't have anything to look back on when you're my age."

Katie leaned forward. "You mean the dream you're holding on to is . . . the past?"

"Well, of course," Mabel Delacorte replied in that deep, almost harsh voice she'd used earlier to keep Katie from leaving the room. "You didn't think I could work up some great dream about my future, did you? No, I'm drawing on the things that were. But sometimes I have regrets. I feel there wasn't enough. I could have done . . . better with my life."

"How?" Katie asked. "I heard you were . . . famous."

Mabel Delacorte smiled. "Hah. That's all relative. More famous than the less famous. Less famous than the more famous. Meantime, I'm afraid I missed out on . . . people. For example, I never told the man I really loved how I . . . felt about him. I was too proud and I lost him."

Katie looked stricken. Was Mabel Delacorte trying to give her some kind of message? Or was Katie just reading her own thoughts into the old woman's words? Maybe Katie *was* being too restrained with Chad.

Their relationship, whatever it was, seemed to have reached a plateau. Katie rapidly began thinking that the next time she saw Chad she'd have to be more open and let him know her feelings. It was a risk, of course. But Katie had to try to have this dream. Even if it didn't turn out exactly as she'd planned, it might still be something to hold on to in *her* distant future.

"There, there," Mabel Delacorte said. She had been watching Katie's anxious expression with concern. "Now I've upset you. Why don't you come and see me next week? I'll be better then. Back to my old self." Mabel Delacorte extended her arm. "But before you go, darling, just hand me that atomizer. The cologne bottle there on the table."

Katie handed the curved glass vial to Mrs. Delacorte.

"Thank you, dear," she said, her voice lighter and almost playful now. "That disinfectant smell is creeping into the room again. One can't have a proper 'dream,' you know, without the right atmosphere."

Going down in the elevator, Katie felt deeply saddened by her visit with Mrs. Delacorte. Before she left today she would try to get Chad's telephone number. Surely Jacqui Beamish would have it. Katie would call him early in the week. She'd start out by telling him about Mabel Delacorte's depression and Mr. Elwood's disappointment. Little by little she'd let him know that she, too, had missed him. . . .

At the main floor, the elevator door slid open and Katie was thrust from her imagined telephone conversation with Chad into the immediate present. Almost directly in front of her in the corridor was Kim Brewer. She was carrying three cans of soda from the vending machine in the lobby and was heading in the direction of the arts and crafts room.

"Ooh," Kim shrieked, "there you are, Katie. We're having such fun over in the crafts room, making all those darling stuffed animals. Come and see."

Katie glanced hesitantly in the opposite direction toward the darkened main lounge. She could hear the movie sound-track scratching and scraping its way toward a noisy conclusion. She guessed that Irma hadn't run into any trouble with the projector after all.

Although it was surely far too late by now to expect Chad, Katie fell into step alongside Kim, wondering briefly who the third can of soda was for. Jacqui Beamish probably, or maybe one of the patients.

A couple of steps short of the open doorway of the crafts room, Kim stopped. She turned to Katie. "Guess what?" she remarked with a challenging look. "An old friend of yours turned up a little while ago. Tracy and I are enjoying the chance to get to know him a little better." She gently waggled one of the cans of soda directly in front of Katie.

Katie's heart gave a resounding thump. The gleam in Kim's eye was unmistakably one of triumph. Katie knew that when she rounded the doorway she would see Chad. And that right beside him would be Tracy Palowski.

CHAPTER
18

Sure enough, Katie was right. Tracy, in fact, was standing very close to Chad. She was showing him a pale blue stuffed kitten, practically poking it in his face, and Chad was looking down at it — at Tracy? — with admiration.

Katie felt a fiery surge of jealousy. Why was Chad so late? And what was he doing with Tracy and Kim in the crafts room?

Chad looked up at Katie and grinned almost sheepishly. Did he feel guilty? Katie hoped so.

"Sorry I'm late," he said, his eyes fixed on her face as she slowly entered the room. She could feel Tracy and Kim watching her, catlike. They were probably enjoying her discomfort, relishing the high color in Katie's cheeks and the feverish glow in her eyes.

Jacqui Beamish glanced up from one of the tables

where she was helping a white-haired resident of the nursing home with her stitching. "I've already told Chad that it's too late today to go up to the patient floors. He thought he might still get in some time with Mr. Elwood."

Jacqui, looking at her watch, sounded definite. It was true that it was nearly four o'clock. The patients' dinner trays began arriving on the floors at four-thirty.

Katie decided to speak up anyhow. She had to find a way of getting Chad to herself so they could talk. "I think he *should* go see Mr. Elwood, even if it's only for a few minutes," she told Jacqui. "Mr. Elwood's very disappointed that Chad didn't come. He was waiting for him. You know how he likes having company. He was really looking forward to this afternoon."

Jacqui appeared thoughtful. Tracy and Kim watched the interchange, their expressions of enjoyment slowly fading. Jacqui consulted her watch again. "Oh, all right then. Better go up this minute, Chad. That movie in the lounge has about ten minutes to run. After that it'll be wheelchair chaos at the elevators." She turned to Katie. "Can Irma manage in there on her own? Shouldn't you be with her her first day?"

Kim tossed Tracy a glance of mild satisfaction at the hint that Katie wouldn't get to follow Chad. Then she thrust the can of soda she'd bought for Chad under his nose. "I got you this. Take it with you?"

Chad paused, slightly surprised. "Oh, uh, thanks," he said, shaking his head in polite refusal. "Maybe Katie would like it."

Katie, already on her way out of the room, turned abruptly at the sound of her name. Chad indicated the drink Kim was holding out to him. "You, Katie?"

Even before Katie began shaking her head in a rapid "no" motion, she could see Kim instinctively withdraw the moisture-beaded can and clasp it possessively to her chest. Imagine, Katie thought, how annoyed Tracy and Kim would have been if she'd accepted their "love" offering to Chad.

Once they were out in the corridor, Chad began to walk more slowly, studying Katie with concern. "Gee, what's wrong, Katie? Are you mad at me?"

"No," she replied, not daring to look at him. Suddenly she stopped walking and forced herself to gaze directly at him. "Well, you *said* you'd be here today. I didn't hear from you last week, but I kept hoping you would come anyhow. Mabel Delacorte's been feeling . . . very down. I guess I'm sort of upset about that and . . . and . . ."

Katie went blank. There was so much she had promised herself she'd say the next time she saw Chad. And now she couldn't manage any of it.

They were standing near the open doorway of a room called the "library." Its walls were lined with shelves of used books and old magazines that were offered around to the patients. There was a large conference table in the center where staff meetings were held. The room was empty.

Chad peered inside briefly, reached out his hand, took hold of Katie's, and drew her inside toward a far corner where they couldn't be seen from the doorway by a casual passerby. Katie pulled away from him.

"What's going on?" he asked nervously. "Listen, I . . . I didn't phone you because I was sure I was coming here today. Then, at the last minute, I had a problem. I had to help out a friend."

Katie watched him, saying nothing, trying to get her own thoughts together.

"I . . . I made it over here as fast as I could," Chad went on. He was still wearing his jacket and a gleam of perspiration covered his forehead. "I left this friend of mine at the vet's with his dog. We should have gone sooner. But we had to go back to my house and get the car. It was . . . complicated."

Katie was taking deep breaths. There was so little time. The movie would end any moment now. Jacqui expected her to be in the lounge. Chad had to get upstairs to Mr. Elwood. How could she possibly ask him outright if he liked her at all? Or even begin to tell him the way she felt about him?

"I have to go this minute," Katie gasped. "Irma, this friend of mine, is . . . is taking care of showing the movie. But she's new here. . . ."

Chad was sitting on the edge of the conference table. He reached out for Katie's hand again. Their eyes met at almost the same level.

"Before you go. Just . . . tell me what got you so upset. Is it something that happened inside there?" Chad nodded in the direction of the crafts room.

With her hand enveloped in his, Katie felt almost faint. "Those girls aren't my friends," she murmured. "I . . . I don't like being around them."

Chad searched her face. He tightened his grip on her hand. "Maybe you mean you don't like *me* being around them. Is that it?"

"Chad, please," she said weakly. "I've got to go."

He shook his head with a determination that surprised her. "You're always running away from me, Katie."

Katie's eyes opened wide. *She* was running away from *him*? How could he say a thing like that?

"You are," he insisted. "You're very businesslike. Sometimes you relax. But other times, you're so . . . serious. You seem like you're all wrapped up in something." Chad scratched his temple. "Gee, I don't know how to figure you out."

Katie looked down at the floor, so shocked at what was happening that she couldn't speak. Chad was accusing *her* of being businesslike, of being too serious, of being hard to know. Those were exactly the things that had been troubling her about Chad. Somehow he had turned the tables on her. Or had she actually been sending him the wrong signals all along?

Katie thought of what Mabel Delacorte had said. She mustn't be too proud to tell the truth. She had already given Chad a wrong impression. Katie with her secrets! She'd done such a good job that Chad Hollister had no idea of her wild, romantic feelings for him.

"It's . . . hard to talk about this," Katie said timidly, but looking directly at him once again. "You and I . . . we never even discussed anything . . . personal. I thought *you* were the one who was always very businesslike. Your work came first. You were so serious. . . ."

Chad shook his head, cutting her off. "That's not true, Katie. And we did talk about personal things. That first time. We talked about . . . having a dream."

Katie tried to gently draw her hand away. "We

never talked about that again, Chad. When you called on the phone, we never even . . . chatted. It was just to set something up."

"Well," Chad stumbled, "because I thought you wanted it that way." He paused, searching for the right words. "It's a good thing we're talking now, though. So we can understand each other from now on."

From now on. There was actually going to be a future with Chad! But there was a condition. Katie would have to tell him how she felt about him, what her dream was. If she had liked Chad only a little, it would have been easy. But she liked him so much more than that. Did he really want to hear the whole truth? Mightn't that scare him away?

"You want me to . . . to admit I got upset about your hanging around with Tracy and Kim just now," she began hesitantly. "To . . . to tell you my feelings. But you haven't told me yours."

Chad let Katie's hand go abruptly. He swung free of the edge of the table where he'd been sitting and began pacing up and back in front of her. He rubbed at his forehead. Suddenly he stopped, his tall figure looming above her. He bent toward her, his voice husky and catching slightly. "I like you . . . a lot, Katie."

Chad's words brought an instant flush to her face. But she tilted her head back to meet his eyes. What she had wanted to tell him came so easily now. "And I *am* jealous," she admitted softly, "because I like you, too, Chad. Very much."

There, she had said it. Enough for a beginning.

* * *

"KAY-TEE!" Her name was being spoken in a loud hiss from just inside the doorway of the "library."

Chad looked over Katie's shoulder, his expression curious. Katie turned quickly. It was Irma. She was beckoning anxiously at Katie.

Irma advanced cautiously into the room. "They're looking all over for you," she whispered. "The movie ended. Jacqui said — " Irma was halfway toward them. Katie's bag with the camera in it, which she had left in the lounge, was slung over Irma's shoulder. "Ah, this must be — "

"Chad," Katie said quickly. "It's lucky you found us first. Jacqui *will* be mad. Chad, this is my best friend, Irma."

Irma put her head, almost coyly, to one side. "You two look . . . just like a picture." Without a moment's hesitation, Irma began digging in Katie's shoulder bag.

Right on cue, she came up with Katie's camera. "Mind if I take a photo of you both? Maybe against that wall. It won't take a minute."

Leave it to Irma, Katie thought, as she went to stand beside Chad, her face wreathed in happiness. This time she'd have the winning picture of the most romantic teen couple *anywhere*!

CHAPTER 19

"Stay for supper, Irma," Katie said on an impulse.

The weather had turned nippy again and they had walked back from their afternoon at the nursing home in a piercing wind under a sky of gray clouds.

"What are you having?" Irma asked suspiciously. She'd been hearing all along from Katie about Zoe's health-food experiments.

Katie shrugged. It was warm and cheerful in the Dinkerhoff kitchen. On the large, round, wooden table between them lay the picture that Irma had just taken of Katie and Chad. Katie kept turning her head to look at it adoringly and to whisper over and over again, "It's a winner."

She turned her attention to trying to answer Irma's question. "What are we having? Hmmm." It was hard to think about food after the brief but

151

wonderful conversation she and Chad had had in the "library" at the Sunnyside. She still couldn't get over the fact that he liked her "a lot," had liked her all along, and had been wondering about her the entire time that she had been so uncertain about *his* feelings.

Discussing the afternoon's events with Irma on the way home, Katie was forced to agree that she had Tracy and Kim to "thank" for having brought matters to a head. If not for Katie's terror of their taking Chad away from her — and her fury at their even trying to — he might never have learned her true feelings that afternoon. It wouldn't have been that easy for Katie to risk her pride and simply blurt out to Chad that she was hopelessly infatuated with him. Even Mabel Delacorte had choked back an important truth when she was young and had sadly lived to regret it.

"I suppose," Katie said dreamily, eyeing the photo one more time, her elbow resting on the table and her cheek nestling in the palm of her hand, "we'll have something of Zoe's for dinner. Maybe her eggplant croquettes. The freezer's full of them."

Irma made a face.

"And a salad with raw pea pods and sprouts," Katie went on absently.

Irma winced.

"I thought you used to like that kind of food," Katie remarked.

"Used to," Irma said. "And I still get it at home until I'm up to here." She drew an imaginary line across her chin. "It's all so healthy you could die from it."

"That's why you've been eating all that steam-table glop from the cafeteria, isn't it?" Katie reflected. "Well, I guess things change. We all change. Only don't laugh. Zoe's eggplant croquettes are a hit. And her gorp cookies, too. She isn't selling that much takeout. But the West Hooperville Deli's given her a standing order every week. Now she's working on getting them to take her zucchini frittata. She may be on to a good thing with this health-food business after all."

"Somebody here talking about me?" Zoe sang out. She breezed into the kitchen. "Why, hello, Irma. I'm real glad to see you."

But Zoe didn't look that glad. In fact, she almost immediately began making nervous little signals to Katie. Katie gave her a puzzled frown. "What *is* it?" Katie whispered, getting up and going over to the sink where Zoe had started washing a basket of greens for salad.

Zoe nudged Katie and pulled away the flap of her skirt pocket revealing a slender piece of mail nestling there. Katie made a grab for it. It was obviously for her and had come in the afternoon delivery. From the Romantic Couples Contest, for sure. How perfect.

Zoe was moving her head from side to side with a small trembling movement, indicating for Katie to be careful of Irma, still seated at the table.

"It's okay," Katie said in a loud reassuring voice. She held up the piece of mail. It was another postcard addressed to K.T. Dinkerhoff from the RCC, with its printed box number in the upper left-hand corner. "Irma knows," Katie declared, approaching the table. "She knows everything."

Irma looked up with a quiet smile. She had understood exactly what was going on from the moment Zoe had started her cryptic signals to Katie. But Zoe hadn't yet known that Irma was in on Katie's secret — on *all* her secrets. And Zoe was a terrible actress.

With a flourish, Katie lay the card down, address side up, next to the photo, which Zoe had not even noticed. "What do you think of this for perfect timing?" Katie exclaimed triumphantly to Irma. "Here's the picture, here's the mail, and all I need now is to write the fifty words about being a couple. Which I think I know a *little* more about since this afternoon."

Zoe, just turning from the sink and hearing the word "picture," lost no time in racing over to the table. "Oh, let me see," she cried out excitedly, frantically drying her hands on a paper towel. She picked up the photo of Katie and Chad and held it close to the giant lenses of her eyeglasses. "So this is Chad," she gasped ecstatically. She turned to Katie. "Oh, darling, he's beautiful. You're both beautiful. Such a romantic couple . . ."

Suddenly Zoe was lifting her glasses and dabbing at her eyes from underneath with the wet paper towel. She reached out jerkily for Katie, threw her arms around her, and embraced her in a tense hug. "Ohh, I feel so bad for you," Zoe gurgled through a fresh onslaught of tears.

Katie pulled back in surprise. What did Zoe mean, "bad?" Irma was looking up at her. "Katie," she said softly, "aren't you going to read what it says on the other side of the card?"

Katie felt a tiny chill across her shoulders, like the sun going behind clouds on a temperamental

154

spring day. Why, it suddenly occured to her, was the Romantic Couples Contest sending her another postcard anyway? When was the entry blank going to come, and wouldn't it be some kind of large sheet of paper in an envelope? With a touch of panic, Katie flipped the card over and started to read it.

Thank you (the printed message began) for your interest in our *Romantic Couples Contest.*

This sounded almost exactly like the first post-card Katie had received. Her eye rapidly skipped along to the rest of the message.

We are sorry to inform you that your request for an official entry blank was received after our contest application deadline of March 15. Please watch for TV, radio, and newspaper releases. The winners in the Teen and Adult Divisions will be announced on August 15. Be on the lookout for future opportunities to find romance and win fantastic prizes.

Katie flung the card down and sent it sliding across the surface of the table in Irma's direction. "Oh, the nerve of them!" she exclaimed as Irma gently lifted the card to read it. "I distinctly remember that I sent in for the entry blank on March twelfth, three days before their deadline, which they never said a word about in the first place. And they even sent me a postcard *saying* they were mailing it." She looked from Zoe (who had already read the card) to Irma with a puzzled scowl. "How can they do a thing like that?"

155

Zoe placed a consoling hand on Katie's arm. "Now, now baby. Those are the breaks. I know how bad you feel, Katie. But you can't fight city hall."

Katie turned to Irma, who was looking up at her with a sympathetic but serious expression. "Why are you so quiet, Irma? You almost look like you knew this was going to happen all along."

Irma was still fingering the postcard. "Well, I did, Katie."

"You did?" Katie challenged. "How? Can you look into the future or something?"

"Oh come on, Katie," Irma said. "I didn't know they were going to refuse you the entry blank. But even if they'd sent it, what chance did you really have of winning? Just figure what the odds are. It's like trying to win the lottery. Aren't you glad now that we didn't waste any time writing those fifty words about being a couple?"

Katie sank down into the chair. "But some people do. Win contests, win lottery money." She reached for the photo of Chad and herself. "And it wouldn't have been such a long shot. We do look . . . romantic."

There was Chad. There was Katie. Side by side. As she gazed at the photo, Chad's voice and the words he had recently spoken reverberated softly in her ears once more. And hearing them, it suddenly came to her, in a delicious moment of realization, that the Romantic Couples Contest no longer mattered in the least. It had "done its job." It had stirred her imagination and transformed her dreaming into action.

She had found Chad and she had centered all her

efforts on him. True, she had never told him how she felt until today. But something of her fierce determination had apparently gotten through to him and made him responsive to her.

When Katie looked up from the photo at Irma and at Zoe, she sensed that they both understood what had just gone on in her head. Chad was important. The Romantic Couples Contest wasn't.

Zoe tapped her on the shoulder. "Come on, cookie. Let's set the table for supper. Irma, you'll stay, won't you? I know that you really enjoy my kind of cooking, even if Katie just picks at it and her parents aren't much better."

A while later they were all seated at the kitchen table polishing off another of Zoe's vegetarian meals, which, Katie had to admit, had been improving.

Babette had come in directly from an afternoon of clothes-shopping and insisted on showing everybody what she'd bought before sitting down to eat. Katie's father had looked on indulgently as Babette held things up in front of her. Her good mood of the past week seemed to be continuing. Katie figured it was best to just accept it and not ask questions.

With Katie's approval, Zoe passed the photo of Katie and Chad around the table.

"Where did you meet this Adonis?" Babette exclaimed.

"His name is Chad," Katie corrected her shyly.

"Looks like a Greek god to *me*," Babette said airily, passing the picture on to Ralph. "Our Katie's growing up," she commented with undisguised pride.

Katie's father studied the photo carefully and

157

looked up, waiting for an answer from Katie to Babette's question.

"I met him a few weeks ago at the nursing home," Katie explained, casting a slightly embarrassed smile at Irma.

Zoe bustled around the table ladling out portions of food. "He's a high-school boy, mind you. And very intelligent. Katie's got good taste."

Babette glanced knowingly at Katie. "Clever of you to borrow my camera. And *very* nice of Irma to take this photo for you." She winked and fell into a discussion with Irma about how she'd liked her first afternoon of volunteering at the Sunnyside.

Everyone chattered amiably for a while. Then Zoe brought out a dessert of carrot cake that was made, she announced proudly, with organically grown carrots.

As if by prearranged signal, Babette began gently tapping her spoon against her water glass. The clinking sound brought the table to silence. "Shall I stand up?" Babette inquired almost timidly of Ralph.

"Of course," he said with a mild grin. "It's your big announcement. Might as well make the most of it."

Babette got to her feet. "I have a secret," she declared with a rather serious air. "Well, Ralph knows it. And Zoe has a little more than an inkling. But the rest of you don't."

That left only Katie and Irma. Katie looked at Irma in bafflement. What on earth was her mother about to tell them? It was a little frightening. Babette seemed happy about her secret. But suppose Katie didn't find the news that wonderful. She glanced nervously at her father. Ralph was leaning back in his chair with his hands clasped behind his head. He looked composed. Or was he resigned?

"Well," Babette said, "I guess I won't drag it out too much. The first thing I have to do, though, is to give credit where it's due. So I want to say that what I'm going to tell you happened all because of Katie."

Katie thrust her hand against her chest and mouthed the word, "Me?"

"Yes," Babette went on. "Katie and I were having breakfast together one morning. I was feeling really depressed about the studio and my so-called career in ballroom dancing. And then Katie said something. At the time it sort of . . . sprang at me and passed over. But then it came back and hit me really hard."

Katie looked around the table. Irma's mouth was partially open, Zoe's glasses were glinting rather sharply, and Ralph hadn't changed his expression.

"What Katie said," Babette continued, "was that I ought to get myself a 'new dream.' That's all. Just two words. But they started me thinking. How about if I got in touch with some of my former contacts in New York City? What about trying to put together an exhibition of ballroom dancing as a theater production? Could I get anybody interested in reviving it as a kind of . . . 'lost art'?"

Babette stopped speaking, her lips pursed in a barely suppressed smile of triumph.

"And you did!" Katie gasped.

Babette nodded and, to Katie's surprise, grabbed for her napkin to dab at the corner of her eye. She sat down looking suddenly emotionally exhausted.

"But what will you be doing exactly?" Katie asked.

She still didn't have a very clear picture of her mother's new undertaking. "When will you be starting?"

"I'll be coaching the company, probably in Manhattan, over the summer. For a fall opening. That's just the outline of the plans that have been discussed over the telephone," Babette answered. She was reviving rapidly. "I'm going down to New York City week after next to iron out details and sign contracts." She leaned across the table and reached her hand out for Katie's. "Guess what? I want you to come with me, Katie. It's Easter Week and you'll be off from school. We'll stay at a hotel right in town. Most of our expenses will be covered by the show's producer. We'll have a ball."

Katie almost recoiled in shock and poked Irma very hard under the table. Things were getting weird — and just a little uncomfortable.

Irma didn't know the exact words that Katie had written down in her diary two days ago for today, March 30. But Katie did.

She had written that she'd gotten a picture of Chad and herself — which she had. And, in a spurt of crazy optimism, she'd added:

New York City, here we come!

CHAPTER
20

"I'm never writing another word in that diary again," Katie vowed.

Irma sighed as she refolded a sweater of Katie's so it would fit into her suitcase better. "I've been hearing that from you all week — ever since your mother asked you to go to New York City with her." It was Sunday afternoon, in Katie's room, and Katie and her mother were scheduled to leave next day on an early-morning flight.

"Do you really think," Irma went on, "that everything you write in that diary of yours is going to just up and happen? After all, the Romantic Couples Contest folded. You thought you were going to be in it and they shut the door in your face."

Katie shook her head stubbornly. "That was just a means to an end. In its own way, it . . . kind of worked. And all the important things *have* come true so far. It's kind of scary. I never thought I'd get my wish about a trip to New York City *this* way. It just shows how tricky those day-ahead diary entries can be."

Irma quietly went on packing for Katie, while Katie sat down on the bed hugging a new pair of designer jeans to her chest. "Every time I talk to Chad I feel worse about spending Easter Week in New York, so far away from him. It's the one time we could really see a lot of each other. And think of all the Tracy Palowskis and Kim Brewers that'll be floating around Hooperville all week."

Irma glanced up and smiled. "Katie, the world's full of competition. You can't hide Chad like one of your old secrets. If he likes you best now, he still will when you come back. Absence is supposed to make the heart grow fonder."

"Or forgetful." Katie took a deep breath. "Oh, I hope not. I hope he remembers to come tomorrow morning to say goodbye to me before we leave for the airport."

Irma gave Katie a serious look. "Did you ever think of telling your mother you didn't want to go?"

"Uh-uh," Katie replied. "I couldn't. You were there, Irma, when she made the announcement. You saw how much it meant to her. She really does feel that I inspired her to start a new dream. And maybe I did. And you know what else she told me? She said she wanted me along for 'moral support.' "

Irma looked surprised. "Your mother always seems so . . . sure of herself."

"Well," Katie mused, "I think this is really a biggie, even for her. Maybe she thinks I have some kind of 'magic.' And maybe she's also trying to sort of make things better between us. We did have our . . . disagreements there for a while."

"Probably this is none of my business," Irma said, "but what does your father think about all of this?"

"He's pleased she's doing it," Katie answered, "even though it means she'll be away most of the summer and the studio will be closed. But he encouraged her to go after the coaching job because she wants to go on teaching and he's been trying to get out of it and build up his insurance business." Katie paused. "I did ask him if he didn't want to go to New York City with her. But he said no. It was her 'baby' and, in a way, mine." Katie shrugged, giving Irma a mildly embarrassed smile. "I guess they're not such a romantic couple after all. You always used to think they were exactly like that pair that was silhouetted on the sign outside the studio."

"That's okay," Irma grinned. "I guess there are different kinds of 'romantic' couples, especially as people get older." She gave a final pat to the clothes she'd packed in Katie's suitcase and spread her hands. "Well, everything looks . . . done. I'll be going, Katie."

Katie looked down at the beautifully arranged case and thought to herself how, ever since Irma had been part of her life, the pieces of her dreams had started to fall into place, too. "I . . . I don't know how to thank you, Irma."

"Oh," Irma said, awkwardly starting to back out the door of Katie's room, "it's nothing. I've always been pretty good at packing. It just comes naturally."

"I don't mean the packing," Katie murmured. "I

163

mean . . . everything. Right from the start. You're the best, most understanding friend I'll ever have. I just hope that I can be . . . as good a friend to you."

Katie put her arm around Irma's shoulder. But, to Katie's surprise, Irma seemed to pull away slightly. Katie couldn't figure out what was wrong.

"Katie," Irma said softly, "there's something I should tell you before I go."

Katie peered at Irma's face. She looked unusually flushed and was grinning sheepishly.

"I met a . . . a boy," Irma said timidly. "In fact, I have a date to . . . to go skating with him tomorrow afternoon."

Katie's eyes opened wide. "You do?" She didn't mean to sound as though Irma couldn't attract a boy. She was certainly looking terrific these days. It was just that Irma had never seemed that interested in dating.

"The thing is," Irma went on, "you might not like him. So don't get mad at me."

Katie burst out laughing. "Oh Irma, how silly. I'm really happy for you. And how could I not like him when I don't even know him."

"That's just it," Irma said shyly. "You do." She paused to take a deep swallow of air. "It's . . . Rob Garrett."

"Rob . . ." Katie couldn't help instantly thinking of all the terrible things he'd said and done. She would never forget that scene in the study hall or that time at the mall. But, oh how glad she was that she'd never told Irma about his having called her "that klutzy-looking friend of yours."

People do change, Katie reflected. They grow and

164

sort of become who they're supposed to be. She herself had changed. Irma had changed. And now it seemed even Rob had changed. It wasn't so surprising after all. Katie had had an inkling of it that day in the lunchroom when she'd told him off and he had awkwardly tried to let her know that his spying on her at the mall had been just a harmless "joke."

"Why, you little . . . secret-keeper!" Katie exclaimed. She had meant it when she said she was happy for Irma. Now they were more than ever on an equal footing. "You didn't have to be afraid to tell me," Katie said. "You can go out with anyone you want. Except Chad." She wagged a warning finger at Irma. "But when I get back you'd better be prepared to tell me *all* the details of how you and Rob got together. And I do mean all."

Katie had a restless night. She was afraid Chad wouldn't be there in the morning to say goodbye to her.

"But we're making such an early plane," Katie reminded him as they'd sat over plates heaped with salad-bar fixings in a pizza restaurant on Friday evening.

Chad shook his head. "I'll really try. If I don't get home too late the night before, I should be able to get up in time."

After turning and tossing for what seemed like hours, Katie fell into a foggy sleep. By the time she woke, it was already past six. Their plane left at eight-thirty and it was a good hour's drive to the airport. She washed and dressed quickly, hearing her parents already stirring around in their room.

Chad had had to drive to a family wedding forty miles away the night before. Would he really get to Katie's house before the sun was up?

Katie padded downstairs, carrying her shoes in her hands and holding her breath. She hastily unlocked the front door and peered out. The street was totally empty. Not a car in sight. Katie's heart sank. There was so little time. Suppose he didn't make it.

She stepped back inside the house to look at the clock in the front hall. It was even later than she thought. Any moment now her parents would be coming downstairs to urge her to have some breakfast with them. There was no way she would be able to eat. But she did go into the kitchen and got down a few sips of orange juice as she nervously listened for the sound of a car outside.

Then, taking a jacket from the rack in the hall, Katie closed the front door behind her and went out onto the porch in her stocking feet. She glanced down the street . . . and there he was! Chad's car — not really his but a sort of second car his whole family shared — was parked a short distance from the entrance to the house, in line with the windows of the studio.

Katie slipped into her shoes and ran to meet him.

Chad flung the door open for her on the passenger side.

"Hi," Katie gasped, unable to control the pounding in her chest. This was such an oddly private time of day to be alone with him. "How long have you been here?"

"Oh, all night," Chad joked, as Katie climbed into the front seat. "Didn't want to take a chance on being late." He turned to face her. "Excited?" he asked.

Katie gulped. "Um-hmmm. At least, I guess I'm excited." She glanced at him out of the corner of her eye. "Of course, it would be nicer if . . . you were going with me."

Chad laughed. "Some chance. Can't you just see the two of us setting off together for the big city?"

Katie gave him a deadly serious look. "Don't laugh, Chad. It could have . . . happened."

Chad appeared disbelieving. "Really?"

Katie shifted around in her seat. "I never told you this," she said almost solemnly. "Maybe you won't even like it. But I tried to get us entered in something called the Romantic Couples Contest, Teen Division. The first prize was an all-expense-paid, fully chaperoned, glamour weekend in New York City."

Chad threw her a look of complete bafflement. "You didn't," he said, his voice actually breaking with surprise. "When was this?"

"Not long ago," Katie replied. She sensed Chad's discomfort. But she had told him too much already to stop now. "The contest closed, though, before I got my . . . uh, our application in. That was why I was running around in circles trying to get a picture of the two of us together." She paused. "For the contest. Well, partly anyway."

"Oh, I see," Chad said, nodding slowly. But Katie felt sure he didn't see. At least, not what she wanted him to.

"Listen," Katie added quickly, "I . . . I don't want you to think I was trying to use you, or anything like that. It *was* part of a dream I had, to go to New York with some wonderful . . . person. But then I met you. Remember that day when we first talked about . . . dreams. I asked you about yours, and I *wanted* to tell you mine. But I . . . couldn't." Katie forced herself to keep looking at him. "I'll tell you now, though. It wasn't really to win that silly contest. My dream was . . . you." She paused just long enough not to lose her courage. "What was yours, Chad?"

Chad gazed at her for a moment and then abruptly looked away. Katie wondered if he was embarrassed. Or was he angry?

He kept on staring out the car window at the houses across the street. Why wouldn't he turn back to Katie? Had she gone too far in confessing about the contest, in telling him her dream, in asking him this? She wanted to tug at his sleeve to make him come back to her. His silence was awful.

"Did I say something wrong, Chad?" Katie asked timidly. "Can't you please tell me?"

Chad shook his head slowly. When he turned to look at her, she could see that he *was* embarrassed. Like that time at the nursing home when Jacqui Beamish had told him that Mabel Delacorte would "go" for him "head over heels."

"Katie," he stammered, "it's not easy for me to talk about . . . some things. I have a hard time telling my . . . feelings."

"But you . . . already did. That day at the Sunnyside. And I told you mine. I was only asking about your . . . dream."

Chad shook his head and looked down at the steering wheel. "Gee, Katie, this is pretty personal."

Katie thought a moment. She supposed dreams *were* terribly personal. Maybe she'd had no right to ask. She was ready to take back the question.

But Chad was nodding slowly. "Okay, okay, if you insist." He tapped on the dashboard nervously. "Everything changed for me a year or so ago, Katie. Before that you wouldn't have known me. I was short and my face was really broken out. I kept my nose in a book most of the time and I didn't date. I was a . . . a nerd."

Katie looked at him in shock. "Oh, Chad, I don't believe you. You're fooling."

"Uh-uh," he assured her. "It's true. I could show you pictures. But I won't. The bad part was that I *felt* the way I looked. I was luckier than some other kids my age. My face cleared up and I . . . grew up." Chad paused. "But the old me, believe it or not, is still locked inside me. You asked about my dream, Katie. My dream was to be able to get a girl *I* wanted interested in me. It still is." Chad looked at her meaningfully. "I hope she'll stay interested."

Katie remained very still, feeling closer to Chad than she had ever even imagined she could. How happy she was that Chad had told her his dream at last. And that she had told him hers.

Later, at the airport with her parents, Katie kissed her father goodbye and then watched him and her mother as they parted.

They *are* a romantic couple, she thought to herself, as Ralph lovingly held Babette's hand in his and she impulsively reached up to kiss him. I'll have to tell Irma she was right about that when I get back.

Katie, meantime, had her own romantic thoughts. She played the final scene of her and Chad in the

169

car over and over again in her mind. She could still see him, sitting in the driver's seat before she left, telling her about himself, talking quietly, and finally leaning toward her and whispering, "Goodbye, Katie. I'll be waiting."

She knew he would.

As the plane lifted off into the sky, Katie smiled and leaned back with a sigh of satisfaction. She was glad that her secret life wasn't a secret anymore. It was an open book.

And she didn't care who read it.

About the Author

The power of positive thinking is what inspired Lila Perl to write *The Secret Diary of Katie Dinkerhoff*. She wondered what would happen if Katie took things a step further than just thinking. If Katie wrote her dreams in her secret diary — could she really make them happen the next day?

Lila Perl, a native New Yorker, lives in Beechhurst, New York with her husband Charles Yerkow who is also a writer. She's written over forty popular books for young people, both fiction and nonfiction. Her books include *Fat Glenda's Summer Romance*, *Marleen the Horror Queen*, and *Junk Food, Fast Food, Health Food*, which was an honor book winner of the Boston Globe - Horn Book Award.